The Mayor of Central Park

Other Books by Avi

The Barn

Beyond the Western Sea, Book I:
The Escape from Home

Beyond the Western Sea, Book II:
Lord Kirkle's Money

Blue Heron

Captain Grey

Devil's Race

Don't You Know There's a War On?

Encounter at Easton

Fighting Ground

The Man from the Sky

The Man Who Was Poe

Night Journeys

Nothing but the Truth
Newbery Honor Book

A Place Called Ugly

Punch with Judy

Romeo and Juliet—Together (and Alive!) at Last

Smuggler's Island

Something Upstairs

Sometimes I Think I Hear My Name

S.O.R. Losers

Tom, Babette, & Simon

The True Confessions of Charlotte Doyle
Newbery Honor Book

"Who Was That Masked Man, Anyway?"

Windcatcher

Tales from Dimwood Forest
Ragweed
Poppy
Poppy and Rye
Ereth's Birthday

Library of Congress Cataloging-in-Publication Data
Avi, 1937–
    The mayor of Central Park / Avi ; drawings by Brian Floca.
        p.   cm.
    Summary: Oscar Westerwit, a squirrel who loves basesball and Broadway
musicals, fights back when a gangster rat named Big Daddy Duds and his
thugs move uptown in the year 1900, invade Central Park, and evict Oscar
and his animal friends from their homes.
    ISBN 0-06-000682-X — ISBN 0-06-051556-2 (lib. bdg.)
    [1. Squirrels—Fiction. 2. Rats—Fiction. 3. Animals—Fiction.
4. Gangsters—Fiction. 5. Central Park (New York, N.Y.)—Fiction. 6. New
York (N.Y.)—History—1898–1951—Fiction.] I. Floca, Brian, ill. II. Title.
PZ7 .A953Me 2003
[Fic]—dc21

                                                          2002154314

Typography by Nicole de las Heras
1   2   3   4   5   6   7   8   9   10
❖
First Edition

For Bill Morris
and
Catherine Balkin

CONTENTS

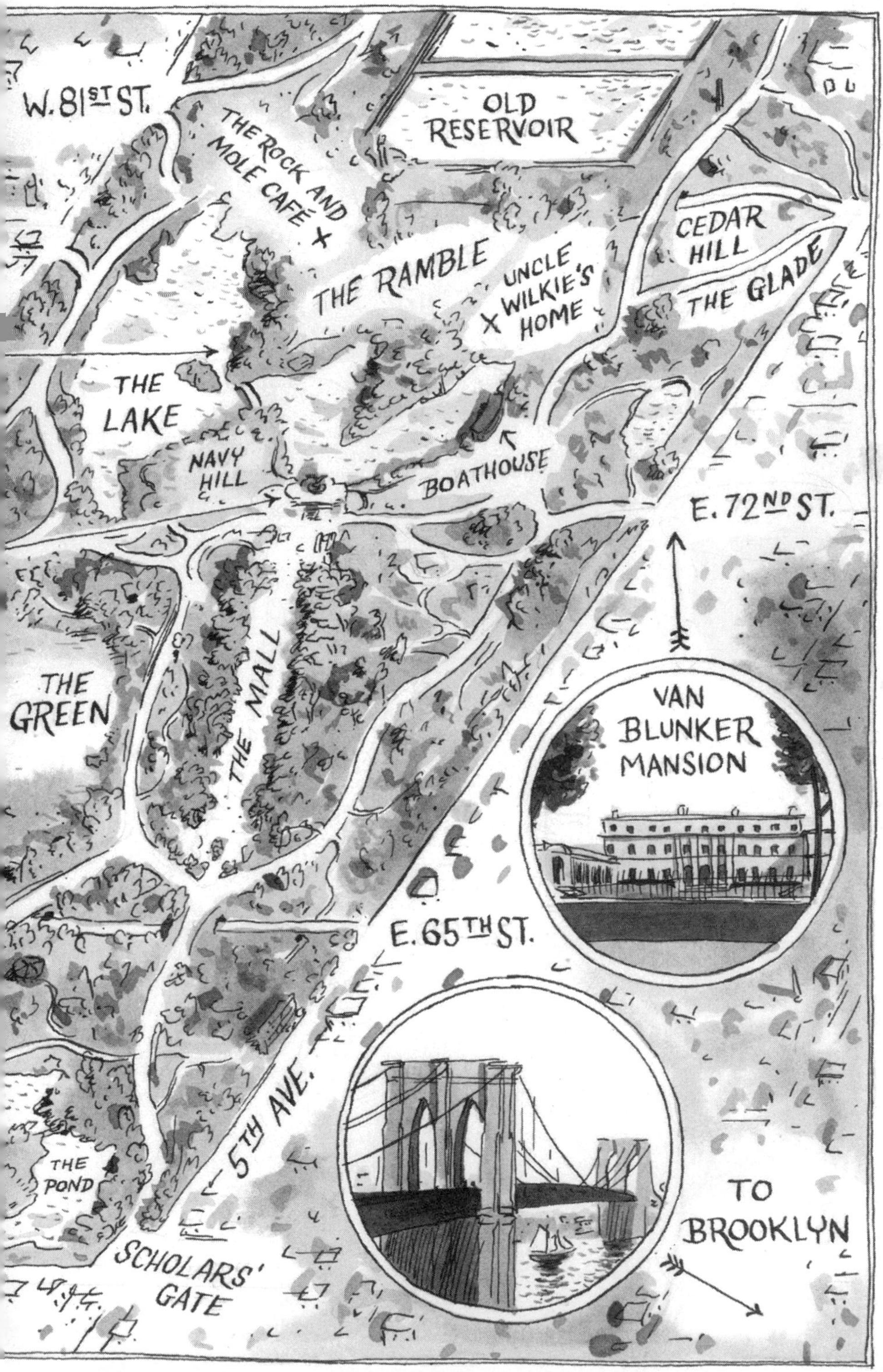

W. 81ST ST.
OLD RESERVOIR
THE ROCK AND MOLE CAFE
THE RAMBLE
UNCLE WILKIE'S HOME
CEDAR HILL
THE GLADE
THE LAKE
NAVY HILL
BOATHOUSE
E. 72ND ST.
THE GREEN
THE MALL
VAN BLUNKER MANSION
E. 65TH ST.
5TH AVE.
THE POND
SCHOLARS' GATE
TO BROOKLYN

The Mayor of Central Park

Chapter the First

I START TELLING THE TALE

Now THE WAY I heard it, this whole loopy story happened in the pearly month of May 1900, right here in the middle of New York City. It's mostly about this gray squirrel who went by the name of Oscar Westerwit.

To look at Oscar Westerwit you might think, hey, just another New York City squirrel. Only thing is, if you said that, you'd be dead wrong. 'Cause the simple scoop is that this here Oscar Westerwit was a full-sized uptown romantic. And when you get an uptown squirrel who's romantic, let me tell you something: You got yourself a story busting to trot itself up Broadway like a tap-dancing centipede.

But you're asking, how come I was able to grab this tale? Well, back in them days I was cub reporter for the *Daily Mirror*. My beat was Central Park. So, figures, while I'm not in the story, I heard all about it.

Anyway, this Oscar Westerwit, this squirrel I'm talking about, the voters in Central Park used to call him the mayor of Central Park. Which ain't to say he actually was mayor. At the time, the real mayor of New York was Hiz Honor Robert A. Van Wyck, a guy so terrific they named a traffic jam after him.

But the thing of it was, since Oscar knew everybody and everything in the park so well, the voters there called him the mayor.

Now to bump right into the beginning, this yarn started spinning string on the third Friday night in May. That was when Oscar held his regular mayor's monthly open house.

Only first you need to fix yourself a picture of Oscar in your head. I mean, this here was one swell-suited squirrel, dressed up to all nine buttons. He was sporting a light, white cotton suit, with a baby blue bow tie, shined-up shoes and spats, and a ripping red gardenia right there on his jacket lapel.

And his home—a two-room elm tree apartment in the middle of the park—was just as terrific. There was an easy chair by the window with an actual electric lamp at its side. There was a pile of *The Baseball Weekly* stacked up along with the New York *Tribune*. Pictures of his heroes—Honus Wagner, Roscoe Conklin, and Lillian Russell—were on the walls, right along with his degree from the City University—class of 1898.

As for Oscar hissclf, he was humming a Broadway show tune and sliding into a tap-dance do-diddle every other step while setting food on the table. You know, like:

> *My sweetheart's the girl in the moon,*
> *I'm getting to marry her soon.*

When all of a sudden, who should come bip-bopping into his room? Sam Peekskill, that's who.

"Hey, Oscar," the rabbit shouted, the way only an excited southpaw rabbit can volume his voice, "Arty Bigalow has gone missing!"

Now what you got to know is, Oscar wasn't just mayor of Central Park. No, sir, he was also the short-stop and manager of the Central Park Green Sox. And a pretty decent player, too.

"Says who?" said Oscar to Sam.

"No one's seen him since day before the day before."

"I'm not worried," said Oscar as he filled a bowl with nuts and crackers and set it by the window.

"How come?" said Sam.

"Sam," said Oscar as he laid out some pretzels and

pickles, "no way Arty's going to miss the game. Hey, if we beat the Wall Street Bulls, we're in first place. He knows that. I know that. Everyone knows that. Here, pal, spot down these cucumber sandwiches."

"Sure," said Sam, doing like he was told. "But Oscar," he said, "this Arty, his personal life is one big spicy meatball. What the guys were thinking was, maybe youse should go check his boardinghouse. I mean, that cat's our only pitcher."

Oscar shook his head and plunked a pile of napkins down like he was flashing a royal flush at a Friday night poker game. "Tonight's my open house."

"So?"

"Hey, Sam," said Oscar. "Come over here."

Sam went to where Oscar was standing by the window.

"See that moon in the sky?" said the squirrel.

"Sure. It's where it's supposed to be, ain't it?"

"Right. But pop your eyes on how the moonlight makes the park hills, lakes, trees, and meadows look like they've been dipped deep in blue light and purple shadow."

"Okay."

"And there—the Dakota towers are looking like servants on the ready. Now—listen to those clip-clopping horses and carriages on Fifth Avenue. And over to the West Side—hear them clanging trolley bells. Got all that?"

"What's all this to do with tomorrow's game?"

"Sam," said Oscar, "this Central Park is . . . perfect."

"Yeah, but if Arty—"

"Hey, pal," said Oscar, "Central Park is where I was born, grew up, and live. Central Park is the best beauty in this whole burg."

"Sure, Oscar, but Arty—"

"Hey, come on. Guys like us have been around here long before 1857 when the park was built; long before the Dutch showed up in 1612. Long even before the Lenape Indians named this island Manna-hata."

"Okay," said Sam. "It's great to know all that stuff, but if Arty don't—"

Oscar spread his forepaws wide. "Hey, I love this place!"

"Oscar," said Sam, "you know where a romantic like youse belongs? In a Broadway show, that's where."

"Broadway Oscar, that's me!" And the squirrel did a quick tap-dance double doodle.

"That's cute, Oscar, but I just hope you're right about Arty."

Wasn't long before the apartment was crowded. Some were there for the nuts, pretzels, and talk Oscar laid out deep. But plenty of folks were there asking for his help.

There was Charley the Choke—a squirrel—looking for a job, any job. There was Mrs. Lydia Frankenfurst— a fox—asking if Oscar could find her slug of a husband a spot in the park sanitation department. There was Mr. and Mrs. Lackawanna—ducks—nervous because their son was spending too much time in East Side pool halls, and him not yet wet beneath the wings.

Oscar offered ears, smiles, and handshakes to them all, promising he'd try and solve their problems.

The high point of the night came late. That was when Mrs. Sissy Nolan called out, "Hey, Oscar, Mr. Mayor, ain't it time for your song and dance?"

That brought an avalanche of applause and cries of "Yeah, Oscar! How about it? Let's hear a song!"

Oscar, grinning big, fetched up his straw hat, held it over his heart, and then, framed by his window and his tail curled over his head, belted out a song in his sweet Irish tenor voice,

> *"O dry those tears, and calm those fears,*
> *Life is not made for sorrow;*
> *'Twill come, alas!*
> *But soon 'twill pass,*
> *Clouds will be sunshine tomorrow;*
> *'Twill come, alas!*
> *But soon 'twill pass,*
> *Clouds will be sunshine tomorrow."*

When Oscar finished the song, he did a quick *rat-tat-tat* soft-shoe *tip-tap* dance, ending up with a fancy, bouncy bow that bent him down to double.

Lots of cheering, you bet.

Anyway, when the open house was over, Sam was the last to leave. "I'm still worried about Arty," he said as he doodled out the door.

"Hey, Sam," said Oscar, "life is lush. There's nothing to worry about."

"If you say so, Oscar. See youse tomorrow at the field."

Alone, Oscar gave himself another peek out the window. The thing is, he *was* excited. The next day's big ball game was a game they had to win. If they did, they'd be in first place and it would be like New Year's Day, Election Day, and graduation day squeezed tight together. And all for the honor of Central Park.

Besides, Oscar knew that Artemus Bigalow—Big Cat they called him—was the best pitcher in the whole Manhattan League. With Arty pitching, they couldn't lose. In fact, Oscar could just see Big Cat sliding that first strike smack over home plate.

"Here's to Central Park and baseball," Oscar proclaimed, tossing his red gardenia out the window for good luck. "Life is an egg-cream sundae with a cherry on top!" Then he clicked his heels twice, flipped his straw hat onto a peg, and jumped into bed.

"I should be in a Broadway show," said Oscar, and fell as sound asleep as a slice of city sidewalk.

Chapter the Second

BIG DADDY DUDS

AT THE SAME time Oscar was sleeping the sweet and simple, way downtown Manhattan, by the Hudson River, a cat, a rat, and a possum got into a rowboat. And what the cat said was, "Mr. Duds, sir, you going to kill me?"

The rat said, "I ain't made up my mind."

The thing of it was, this here cat was none other than Artemus Bigalow himself, Oscar's one-and-only pitcher. He was dressed in a sporty blue jacket, paper collar and dickey, bow tie, high shoes, and a brown derby. I mean, he looked like he was perked and parked for a pretty swell party. Except for two things: His paws were tied together, and he'd been forced to sit in that rowboat.

And who forced him? It was the rat, that's who. And who was this rat? It was none other than Dudley Aloysius Throckmorton, better known around New York as Big Daddy Duds.

This here Big Daddy Duds was a big-chested rat, with a sharp, hairy snout, beady eyes, and real small ears. He also had a long tail—naked.

A diamond stud was stuck to his red cravat. In fact, there were diamond rings popping all over his paws. But then, Duds was a big-time jewel thief. Which helps to explain why, in the right pocket of his coat, was a pistol bulging big with bullets.

Aside from this getup and gat, Duds was a baseball nut. He was always wearing a baseball cap with the letter *B* on it. This *B* stood for the National League baseball team the Brooklyn Superbas.

As for the fat possum rowing the boat cross the Hudson, he went by the name of Uriah Pilwick. At the time this all happened, Pilwick was already pretty old, with posture that would have made a pretzel squeak with envy. His whiskers were gray. His eyeglasses were thick as sarsaparilla bottle bottoms. A long, brown overcoat reached his ankles. A derby squatted on his head.

Anyway, these three guys were rolling cross the

Hudson River, and at first, no one was saying nothing. The water was all hard chop and soft fog. Few stars could be seen. Shore lights were dull. Not much could be heard save a few buoy bells banging. But believe me, Artemus Bigalow was one fearful feline.

So after a while he said, "Hey, Duds, how come you're doing this to me?"

"Bigalow," said Duds, "wasn't for you, I could have gone to the ball game. Instead, I took my time tagging you."

"I'm sorry," said Artemus.

"I'm sure you're sorry," said Duds. "Didn't I tell you to keep away from my daughter?"

"Yes, but . . ."

"Don't butter me no buts. You were just about to marry up with her, right?"

Artemus blinked. "How'd you know?"

Duds glanced at Pilwick. "I got ways of knowing."

"Sir," said Artemus, "Maud and I love each other. I even taught her to pitch my best pitches."

"Lob no love lip at me, pal," said Duds. "Love is for baseball. Next to diamonds, it's the best thing in the world. Baseball is a beautiful game, Bigalow, like you already knows. But, like most everybody also knows, youse ballplayers are a bundle of bums. And let me tell youse, no daughter of mine is going to marry no bum. As for teaching a doll to dish a pitch, you might as well teach a brick to be a banana."

"Then I'll stop loving Maud," the cat said.

"Bigalow, that remark totals two things: the size of your heart and the size of your brain. Pea size—the both of them."

"Mr. Duds," the cat pleaded, "I'm a good pitcher. The best in town. I throw a knuckleball-spitball combo that floats to the plate like a nervous butterfly with a history of hiccoughs. It's that hard to handle. In fact, I have a game tomorrow morning I can't miss. For the Central Park Green Sox."

"Bigalow, I know all about youse. You're good. Very good. Too bad youse had to throw curves round my daughter. Can't have that."

The cat looked away.

"Bigalow," said Duds, "we're halfway to Jersey. You got some choice choices to choose. So lock your lip and clear the ears. Here's my pitch: I could drill you. I could drown you. Or I could toss you a thousand bucks. What's the call?"

"I'd kinda like to catch the cash."

"Sure thing, Bigalow, but if I chop you coin, you got to swear to never noodle near my daughter no more. What's more, you got to take the dough and deal yourself a one-way horse to California. First class, second class, don't matter to me, long as it's got four legs. And the thing is, no balks. You got to stay there."

"Mr. Duds," said Artemus, "there ain't no big-league baseball teams out west. Couldn't I just drift uptown?"

"Bigalow, that's as funny as a one-dollar bill on a two-dollar IOU."

"I'm serious, Mr. Duds," said Artemus. "Downtown is down. But uptown is up. It's where you should be."

Duds popped his pistol from his pocket. "Maybe you're right, Bigalow, but you've already got two strikes. One more, you're out. 'Less you hit me some distance, you're dead as a dodo on Delancey Street."

"Mr. Duds, sir," said Artemus, quick as a jaywalker in Times Square, "I don't fancy being folded."

"Okay. But if you takes my coin and cross me off, I'll still kill you, Bigalow. 'Til it hurts. Understan'?"

"Yes sir."

"All right, then, we done a deal. Keep rowing," he said to Pilwick.

The possum pulled the oars.

Chapter the Third

DUDS DOES SOME THOUGHTS

So URIAH PILWICK guided the rowboat near to Jersey. With a nod from Duds, the possum cut the ropes that bound the cat.

"Okay, cat," said Duds, "dog-paddle time."

Bigalow didn't dicker. He dove from the boat into cold water that numbed him from his knees to his nose. His derby drifted north. Spats and shoes went south. By the time the cat got to shore, he was shivering so bad his knees were banging like the bells atop St. Bart's.

Even so, the cat had enough tin to call, "Hey, Duds, what about my dough?"

"Oh, yeah," said Duds. "Your go-west wampum." He nodded to the possum. "Go on. Give it to him."

"Okay, Boss." So Pilwick winked a one-hundred-dollar bill from his coat pocket, rowed closer to the shore, and offered it to the cat on the oar blade tip.

"Mr. Duds, sir," said the dripping Bigalow, grabbing the bill, "this is a hundred. I believe you talked a thousand."

"Bigalow," said Duds, "if I thought you really loved my daughter, it'd be a thousand. But it ain't her youse love. It's my money you're mooching. Maybe youse pitch perfect, but mostly, youse a punk. You're lucky I'm donating a dime. Now, beat it." With that Duds aimed his pistol at the moon and wiggled the trigger. At the big bang, Bigalow galloped into the Jersey bog.

Duds sighed. "Hey, Pilwick, thanks for letting me know that dumb cat was going to mosey off with my money and my Maud."

"It's my job to know what to know when it's worth the knowing, Boss," said the possum.

"Yeah," said Duds. "Far as I can tell, what you don't know ain't happened yet. You and me, we're as close as crossed fingers in a buttoned-up mitten."

"Thanks, Boss."

"So let me tell you from my insides, daughters are disasters. A son, he'd have been a real ballplayer."

"If you say so, Boss," said the possum.

"As for you, Pilwick: You've only got one error."

"What's that, Boss?"

"You root for the New York Giants."

"Boss, I'm a Manhattan possum."

"Too bad. It's a mistake. The Brooklyn Superbas is the only.* Thing is, Pilwick, when you have an error like that inside, you might go limp like a lousy lily outside. Just know I'm keeping my eyeballs on your buttons. Now, come on," he growled. "Back to town. I've got some thought that I needs to think."

"Sure thing, Boss."

So the possum manned the oars while the rat mulled his mind. But as they got close to Manhattan, Duds looked up and said, "Pilwick, I've made up my brain."

"What's that, Boss?"

"That Bigalow was a bum. But he said right. Downtown ain't good enough for me. The gang should move uptown. There'll be more jewels to grab. Maybe enough to buy me a ball club."

"Think so?"

"Hey, Pilwick, am I a jewel thief or am I a jewel thief?"

*Just in case you were wondering: This all happened before the American League (and the Yanks) were invented.

"You're a jewel thief."

"So, if there's a better diamond than a baseball diamond, I don't know its name," said Duds.

"Whatever you say, Boss," said Pilwick.

"I did say," said Duds.

Chapter the Fourth

OSCAR'S BIG GAME

Now, REMEMBER THAT game that Sam and Oscar were talking about? Central Park Green Sox against the Wall Street Bulls? Okay. It was set to start Saturday morning, eight o'clock sharp as scissors.

Oscar's alarm clock went loud at six. He bonked out of bed, pulled on his boxers, did some barbell basics, then stuffed down a breakfast of nuts and eggs. By six forty-five he was in his green uniform, heading for the field. He had his bat on his shoulder and his glove on his belt. The glove was pretty small, not like them butterfly nets they call mitts today. Oscar also brought along a rake to smooth down the baseball field.

After plucking pebbles from the base paths, he made sure first, second, and third bases were bright and tight. He washed home plate 'til it sparked like a Ritz-Carlton platter.

Once the infield was set, Oscar ran laps around the outfield and took some practice swings. In his head, he went the whole circuit: a single, double, triple, home run. Not just that either. He made all twenty-seven outs.

After that, there was nothing to do but wait 'til both teams trooped.

First to come was Sam Peekskill. Oscar's rabbit friend was not just the right fielder but, being a pretty hefty hare, led the team in home runs with six, which was tons in them days before Babe Ruth. Then came Parker Baladoni, a mutt, as well as Cyrus X. Furdly, a long-necked swan (known as Stretch), who used it to play first base. Big Benny Ludwig, a red squirrel, and Ulysses Simpson Crackover, a fox, better known as Reds, followed. Reds was the catcher. There was also Canfield Roach, third baseman. The last to show was Engelbert Maxamillion, the mouse left fielder who, despite his name, couldn't keep a penny in his pocket if it were pinned there.

Oscar greeted them all with slaps on backs. "Great to see you, pals!" After which the team warmed up.

Park fans began to show too. They were pretty

excited. Oscar even did his mayor's bit by shaking a few loose palms.

"Hey, Mr. Mayor, going to give us a song?" someone in the crowd called out.

"If we win, I will," said Oscar, with a willing wink and a quick-foot one-two, one-two, which made the crowd rip out a roar. Oh, sure, Oscar was pretty chipper.

It was only when the Wall Street Bulls began to appear that he noticed Artemus Bigalow hadn't shown.

"Pop a pocket," he muttered. "Where's Big Cat?"

The umpire—a puffed-up East Side, pigeon-toed pigeon—called out, "Play ball time."

Trouble was, Artemus Bigalow still wasn't there.

"Think he forgot the game?" Oscar asked Reds.

"Doubt it," said Reds. "Three nights ago, when I was over to his place, we goes through the whole Bulls lineup. You know, how to pitch this one, that one. He knew the game then."

"Hey, Oscar," the umpire called, "you guys ready to play or what?"

"Our pitcher ain't here," said Oscar.

"Too bad," piped the pigeon. "Either the game gets going or it gets gone."

Oscar checked with his other teammates, asking them if they knew about Artemus.

No one knew nothing.

Oscar went to the Bulls manager. The big black

squirrel was named Archibald Cornwallis, better known as Corny. A good pal of Oscar's, he was sympathetic.

"Won't be much of a game if you guys only got eight players," said Corny.

"And he's our best pitcher."

"He's your only pitcher," Corny pointed out. "Hate to have you forfeit."

"What about postponing 'til next week?" asked Oscar.

"Sure," said Corny.

So Oscar made the announcement to the crowd, which, though disappointed, hiked on home.

"Any of you guys know where Artemus lives?" Oscar asked as his team was heading off.

"Lower East Side," said Reds. "Four-twenty-two Avenue B. A boardinghouse."

So Oscar—still garbed in baseball gear—dropped a jitney (otherwise known as a nickel) on the horse trolley and took himself downtown to a four-story brownstone building with a sign in a window:

> # ROOMS RENTED
> # ⇥ TO ⇤
> # REFINED GENTS

Oscar gave a yank to the bell rod. Wasn't long before an old lady peacock opened the door. She was a big old bird with rouge on her cheeks and a powdered beak. Wide in the chest, she had enough jangling necklaces round her neck to wake the town New Year's morning. Her tail feathers were big enough to fan the world.

"Yes?" she asked, holding a pair of glasses to her small black eyes.

"Madam," said Oscar, "I'm after Arty Bigalow."

"What are you, some friend or something?"

"I'm the mayor of Central Park and the manager of the Central Park Green Sox, the team he plays for—that's who."

"Bigalow ain't home," said the peacock. "He was in three nights ago with some friend. Then he went out with Mr. Pilwick, one of my gent boarders. That was the last time I seen him."

"Any idea when he might be coming back?"

"Mister, this place, you mind your own business."

"Sure," said Oscar, "but if you see him, tell him his teammates were asking."

Oscar took the trolley back uptown. *Where the ketchup,* he wondered, *is that cat? How could he miss such an important game?*

Chapter the Fifth

DUDS PLOTS HIS PLAN

JUST ABOUT WHEN Oscar was beating it back to Central Park, Duds was holding a meeting with his gang about where to move uptown. And of course, what do they come up with? You guessed it—Central Park.

"What makes you lugs think this here Central Park is so perfect?" asked Duds.

"It's big, grassy, and mostly empty," said one of his lieutenants. "Best clump of green going."

"It's got this Mall, Boss," said another, "long and wide, which goes right into the park. Full of trees. With leaves, even. And this here Mall leads to a terrace, which has an angel on it. Got a place for your office right there. And, get this, Boss, there's a lake. With water."

"Keep talking," said Duds.

"Better than all that, Boss," said another lug, "this terrace is where all the uptown nib-nobs go to show their jewels. Be so easy to do stickups, we'll all be millionaires by last Thursday."

"I could grab that," said Duds.

"But here's the bestest part, Boss," said another rat. "There are gobs of baseball fields. There's even a team. The Central Park Green Sox. They play in the Manhattan League."

"Hey," said Duds, "this place sounds sassy. I've been wanting a team of my own. Anyone living there?"

"Just a few."

"What kind of few you talking?"

"Birds. Chipmunks. Mice. Rabbits. The usual. But mostly squirrels."

"Don't worry. Them types will show tail long before they show fight. Lousy ballplayers, too, the whole squad of 'em. How many squirrels you figure?"

"Scads."

"And they think the park belongs to them," said another rat.

"Hey," said Duds, "I never met an animal I couldn't turn his tale. We'll take care of 'em all."

"How we going to do that?" said another rat.

"See, what we do," said Duds, "is get into this

here park, fast. At night. No warnings. Just go in, see. Once we're in, we're in. Then they has to get us out. Understan'? Anyone gets in our way—we roughs them round a bit. Or we gets rid of them. That way, no hard feelings."

"Okay, Boss. Whatever you say."

"I am saying," said Duds. "Mind, we'll only take part of it at first. See how things happen. After that . . . who knows?

"And here's what else we do: When we goes—in two days—all you guys pack heat. On the outside. Anyone sees the gats you got, they know the trouble they'll get."

"What if them animals go to the cops?" asked one of the lugs.

Duds grinned a grin that had more teeth than a toothbrush. "Don't clutter your brain about no cops. The new police commish—Titus Snibly—is one of my pals. I own the guy. And he's a Brooklyn booster too."

As soon as the meeting was over, Duds turned to Pilwick.

"Okay then. We set?" Duds asked.

"Sure thing, Boss," said Pilwick. "But what about your wife and daughter? You letting them know?"

"Yeah. I suppose I should," said Duds. And he headed for home.

Chapter the Sixth

DUDS IN HIS DIGS

DUDS LIVED IN a twelve-room apartment down on Charlton Street. The rooms had high ceilings and were stuffed with more furniture than a warehouse. All of it was big and heavy stuff, like Duds. Chandeliers hung from the ceiling like melting icicles. Windows drooped with colossal curtains and tons of tassels. On the walls, oil paintings of fruit and sunsets, you couldn't tell which. On the floor, Turkish carpets laid low.

Okay, so when Duds got there, his wife—her name was Bertha—was setting back on the parlor couch looking at the *Ladies' Home Journal* and imbibing chocolate bonbons. She dressed in style: bunches of black silk and satin with a corset that kept her waist like an hourglass squeeze.

Anyway, Duds came in, dumped himself into a chair, crammed a cigar into his mouth, and started to stink the room.

No one said nothing 'til Bertha, after crushing another chocolate in her mouth, spoke: "Duds, my life is dull."

"Is that right?" said Duds.

"Remember when we were young?"

"Bertha, I'm so busy I forgets to remember."

"Duds, we used to trip the light fantastic," his wife said. "Now all we do is fan the light."

"You got a nice apartment, don't you?" said Duds. "I gets you chocolates and diamonds, don't I? You go to the opera, right?"

"Sure," she said. "You swipe the diamonds, and the chocolate is stale and cheap. As for the opera, it's once a week and just with Maud. Besides, I don't understand one word. They sing foreign. For you," Bertha said, "life is just stealing things and going to ball games. For you, love is lost."

"I love diamonds," said Duds, plopping ashes onto the floor. "And I got only so much love in me."

"Don't you love me?"

"Bertha, for you my sentiments is mostly sentimental."

"Maud loves being a nurse," Bertha said. "You say no to that."

"Hey," said Duds, "working girls don't work for me. My daughter needs to get married, have kids, and eat chocolates. Be content. Like you."

"Then let her marry Artemus Bigalow," said Bertha. "He says he loves her. These days she thinks she's loving him. Then you'll have a son who's playing ball. What more can you ask?"

"Actually, that Bigalow is a bum trying to catch my cash," said Duds. "Which is why I just stuffed him with cheap coin, which he took and went. Maud ain't going to see him never again. Which reminds me: We're moving too."

"Where?"

"Uptown. Central Park. The Mall. Right off Fifth Avenue. Swellest place in town."

"The whole thing?"

"We can start small. Move to more."

"Why?"

"It's classier. Got more jewels to grab there than anywhere. Be better for Maud, too. She can have herself an uptown husband. I'll make me some dough and get myself a ball team."

"When?"

"Soon."

"Who?"

"The gang. Everybody. The whole kit and caboodle."

"Duds," said Bertha, "I'm a downtown rat. I'll get no moxie from moving uptown."

"We're moving, Bertha," Duds bellowed. "In two days. Soon as the moon is full."

"Duds, I'm not daffy with this."

"Bertha," said Duds, "I'm not talking happy. I'm talking going."

"Don't you think you should tell Maud?" said Bertha.

"You tell her. I got a game to see. Brooklyn 'gainst the Pittsburgs. Should be the ant's uncle."

And Duds left the house.

Chapter the Seventh

MISS MAUD

SO WHAT HAPPENS next was Bertha binged two more bonbons, then beat it back to her daughter's room.

Now the thing of it was this Maud Throckmorton was a whole different package than her pop. For one, she kept her room simple. Just a narrow bed, a pinewood bureau, a straight-back chair. On the bureau was this picture of Artemus Bigalow, looking Mr. Cool Cat in his Central Park Green Sox baseball suit.

As for Maud, she was a slim young rat wearing a new nurse's uniform: long, black sleeves and ankle-length dress. A white apron covered her dress and was tied to the middle of her chest. A white cap was on her head. On her feet were high-button shoes.

When Bertha came in, Maud was packing a small carpetbag with clothes and medical books.

"Maud, baby," said Bertha, "what you doing?"

"Mama," said Maud, "I've got news for you."

"Me too," said Bertha. "You first."

"Mama," said Maud, "Artemus Bigalow wants me for a wife. I said sure, so we're hitching up. Except . . ." Maud picked up the picture of the cat.

"Except what?"

"Ma, I ain't too sure he loves me. Sometimes I think it's just Pa's cash he wants to cozy. In fact, I ain't seen him these past few days. That kind of wooing feels worse than wrong."

"Maud," said Bertha, rising up and offering the chair. "Better you sit. My news is worse even more."

"Which is?"

"Bigalow is gone."

"Ma!" cried Maud. "That true?"

"Your pa sent him packing."

"Why?"

"Just what you said: The cat was only poking into his pile."

"How did Pa know?"

"Your pa gave him some money and he melted."

"Where did he go?"

"Don't know."

Maud took a deep breath and then said, "Ma, I was moving uptown before. I'm still going to take the hike."

"Why, baby?"

"It's time I strung my own beads."

"Your pa says we're also moving."

"Where?"

"Same place. Uptown. Said you could find yourself a decent husband there."

"I'm wasted wanting husbands. It's time for something else. When are you moving?"

"In two days."

"I'll go first," said Maud.

"Is my baby's heart broken?" asked Bertha.

Maud held her head up high. "Ma, I've got my pride. I don't like Pa keeping my life pickled in his pocket."

"He's your father, babe."

"Mama, he cares for just two things: money and baseball."

"Sweetheart," said Bertha, "just know that no matter what, your mama loves you. Want to know where we're moving?"

Maud shook her furry head. "Ma, we can always meet at the opera, Tuesdays at seven-thirty."

"You don't like the opera."

"But I love you," said Maud.

Now the thing is, soon as Bertha got back to her own room, she sat down at her writing desk, picked up a pen, and wrote a private note to Uriah Pilwick.

Uriah—
Please come see me immediately.
                            —Bertha

As for Maud, she stared at the picture of Artemus Bigalow for a long time. "How could a babe as smart as me be so dumb?" she asked herself.

She reached into her carpetbag and pulled out a baseball. Artemus Bigalow had signed it.

Maud—I'm making a pitch for you—Arty

Maud sighed and wiped away a tattered tear. Hard to say which she was more, dusted or determined.

Chapter the Eighth

OSCAR WORRIES

NOW UPTOWN, 'BOUT the same time, Oscar was getting really worked about Artemus Bigalow. After all, the cat was still gone and no one knew the why or how. There wasn't just one rescheduled game with the Wall Street Bulls, either. There was a Wednesday afternoon game against the West Side Worthies. There were also games set against the East Side Elites, the Harlem Hotspurs, and the Bowery Bums.

Oscar was beginning to think they'd have to forfeit them, too.

So what he did was, he tootled another trolley trip

to the Lower East Side and the rooming house where Big Cat was supposed to be napping. But all the land-lady would tell him was that Bigalow had not alighted lately.

"Have you thought of calling the cops?" Oscar asked, stepping aside to let a pokey possum pass out through the door.

"You saying there's been foul play in my boarding-house?" said the peacock.

The words made Pilwick—the possum—stop at the bottom of the stoop and listen.

"Lady," said Oscar, "I'm not suggesting nothing. I'm just worried. Bigalow isn't just a friend, he's my teammate. And he's missing. We've got games to play."

"Humph!" said the peacock as she triple-sized her tail. "If I had known he was a ballplayer, I'd never have let him rooms. I only rent to decent gents. Besides, he owes me two weeks' rent. Who's going to pay?"

Oscar, none too happy, hopped off.

As for Pilwick, he watched Oscar as he went, not that the squirrel noticed.

Back in the park, Oscar met with Sam so they could figure out what might have happened to the cat.

They met in The Rock and Mole Café. This here café, which was right in the middle of the park, was a dive Oscar often sat in with friends. Inside was a long, low room with a low, rock ceiling and a few low-wattage electric bulbs. A low place for sure. The smell of the underground mixed with food, drink, fur, and feathers made it homey. On the wall were framed pictures of Pete Stuyvesant, Freddy Olmsted, and Teddy Roosevelt. There was also a picture of an old baseball team, the Downtown Dutchmen.

On one side of the room was a long counter. Behind the counter was a big mirror and a shelf with colored bottles and jugs. Stools were set before the counter.

Polishing glasses behind the counter was a mostly blind mousy mole who went by the name of Molly. A long time ago, she played right field for the Downtown Dutchmen. Now, a white apron was tied round her ample waist.

"Do you think Arty left town?" Oscar asked Sam as they drank a glass of flat sap.

"Don't know," said Sam.

"Want to know what I heard?" said Molly from behind the counter.

"Sure," said Oscar, who knew that the blind mole knew much and noticed more. Sure enough, Molly said, "The word is Arty has this hang-on-his-arm, you know, a girlfriend. And guess what, she's a gangster's daughter."

"A gangster!" cried Oscar.

"Big Daddy Duds—the boss of downtown himself," Molly went on. "Arty was planning to marry up with this girl. But the way I heard it, it wasn't no love for the lady that led him loony. It was her father's loot."

"He's a great pitcher," Oscar said, shaking his head.

"But to hitch yourself to a gangster's daughter just for her father's scratch—you can't sing much of a song for that."

"You got a better reason?" asked Sam.

"Hey," said Oscar, "what's the matter with love?"

"Maybe he skipped town before he got married," said Molly.

"But what are we going to do for a pitcher?" Oscar asked.

"You're the manager," said Sam.

"And," added Molly, "you're the mayor, too."

Oscar sighed. He didn't feel too full of chips or chirps.

Chapter the Ninth

MISS MAUD MAKES HER MOVE

So what happened next is Big Daddy Duds told his gang that, having arranged for a big bright moon, they'd move uptown the next night. He told Bertha. She told Maud. Maud, on the quick and ready, gave her ma a hasty hug, heaved a few more hankies into her bag, and hurried out the door.

Only thing is, no sooner did she bolt from the building, when who should be there but the old possum himself—Uriah Pilwick.

"Good morning, Miss Maud," Pilwick said, dipping his derby. "Are you running away?"

Maud, knowing how tied the possum was to her pop, came to a hasty halt. Truth is, she was scared. But being her father's daughter, she also stood tough. "How did you know what I'm doing?" she said.

"Miss Maud," said the possum, "it's my job to know what to know when it's worth the knowing."

"You going to tell my old man?"

"Miss Maud, your pa and I don't agree on everything. Instance: He roots for the Brooklyn Superbas. I go for the New York Giants. I'm just hoping your love ain't tied too tight to Arty Bigalow."

Maud held her head up high. "Mr. Pilwick, do you know where Mr. Bigalow was bounced?"

"Last time I seen him," said the possum, "the cat was wet and working west. There were no shoes on his feet, but there were a hundred clams in his claws."

"Can you find him?"

"Miss Maud, Bigalow's love for you was lousy. It was your father's lolly he liked."

"What makes you so sure?"

"He told me. We bunked in the same boardinghouse over to Avenue B."

Maud blanched. But all she said was, "He was dashing."

"Only now, Miss Maud," said Pilwick, "he's dashing away."

Maud swallowed hard and licked her lips.

"Miss Maud," said Pilwick, "what you going to do?"

"I'm a nurse. I'll do that."

"Let me wish you lobs of luck. Just know, Miss Maud, if you ever need help, you can look to me."

"Thank you, Mr. Pilwick," said Maud. "But it's time I dropped my own dime." That said, Maud held her head high and walked away.

Feeling like an uptown trolley on a downtown track, Pilwick watched her go. Then he tottered back to his rooming house with his tail dragging and his shoulders stooping.

The possum's room had nothing but an iron bed, a desk, and a chair, plus a porcelain washbasin. The shared bathroom was down the hall and up too many steps. On Pilwick's wall was a pair of pictures. One was the New York Giants baseball club. The other was Miss Maud herself. Underneath the picture of Maud was a vase with violets. Each day, for years, Pilwick had replaced them. The thing of it was, Pilwick had a long love for Miss Maud.

Mostly miserable, the old possum plumped down on his bed and peered at his pictures. The Giants were in last place. Maud was moving on. Life seemed lost and lousy. Pilwick had more grief piled up than the tallest building in town.

"I've done wrong too long," Pilwick said to himself. "It's time I done some good."

So what the possum did was take up pen and paper and write:

> Dear Mr. Wolfgang Van Blunker,
>   In the past we were pals and I favored you with some favors. You said if I ever needed something back, I should ask. I'm asking now.
>   What I need is . . .

Pilwick took himself to a Western Union office and tootled off his telegram. Then he went back to his room and packed what was his so he could move uptown with Duds.

Finally, he said good-bye to his landlady. This peacock had no joy that the possum was parting. Not that the old possum noticed. But then there's this old saying that says a busted heart boasts its own grief best.

Chapter the Tenth

WHAT HAPPENED TO MAUD

NOW IT DIDN'T take long for Maud to figure out that she needed a place to live and to work. So she bought herself a newspaper, poked through the help wanted pages, and found an ad that read:

MISS MALDOON'S NURSING AGENCY
THE ONLY ONE IN NEW YORK CITY!

Positions Always Available for Suitable Young Women
357 14th Street · Suite 12

Now as I heard it, this here agency was in a small office on the sixth floor of a large office building. Maud took a creaky elevator up and went to suite twelve. What she found was an ostrich sitting behind a desk, a telephone by her side.

"Please," said Miss Maud, "I'm pitching for a nursing post."

"Young lady," the ostrich replied, "you've come to the right place. I merely need to know if you're acceptable."

"I'm willing to accept anything," said Maud.

"That's good enough for me," said the ostrich. "May I ask where you studied nursing?"

"Over to St. Luke's," said Maud. "Got myself a city certificate."

"Better to better. My name is Miss Lulu Maldoon," said the ostrich. "What's yours?"

"Maud Throckmorton."

"Miss Throckmorton," said Miss Maldoon, barely batting her big eyes, "at the present moment I have no hospital appointments. The only job available is a private placement with a wealthy old goat that stays at home. He needs companionship as well as some simple attention. The position pays twelve dollars a month plus room and board. If you prove suitable to my client, you could start at once."

"Sounds smart to me," said Maud.

"Excellent," said Lulu Maldoon, and she offered a card.

"Present this with our compliments at Seven-ninety-eight Fifth Avenue. Ask for Mr. Van Blunker. There is no fee. If he finds you fine, he shall pay me first."

"Thanks a wad," said Maud. And taking the card, she took off.

Now, soon as Maud left, Miss Maldoon picked up the phone and rang on through.

"Mr. Van Blunker," she said, "this is Lulu Maldoon. As we hoped, Maud Throckmorton was just here. I've directed her to your home. Always pleased to be of service," she said before ringing off.

Wasn't long before Maud was standing before 798 Fifth Avenue, which was near Seventy-second Street. What she saw was a monster mansion that looked down on the avenue as if it owned it. The windows were wide. The doorway was wider. Not that Maud cared. All she wanted was a place to bunk and work.

She pushed the doorbell. After a couple of minutes, the door was opened by a turkey in a servant's uniform.

"Yes, please?" said the turkey, red wattles working with every word she whistled.

"My name is Maud Throckmorton. I'm here for the nursing post." Maud handed over the card that Miss Maldoon had given her.

The turkey barely glanced at it. "Ah yes," she said. "We were expecting you. My name is Evelina Telesforo, sole servant. Please trot along with me."

Maud followed the turkey down a carpeted hallway

lined with fancy furniture and so many old paintings on the walls she couldn't see the walls. These pictures were, she guessed, rich and dead ancestors. What's more, the hallway had heaps of newspapers, books, and milk bottles scattered everywhere. It was a major mess.

They went into a large parlor with more pictures on the walls, more books on the floor, and more floor covered with papers.

Sitting on a large couch was this old goat. He was dressed in a fading Chinese silk robe, and patched patent leather slippers. A wispy, white beard wiggled from his chin. His yellow horns were crumpled with age. His pale eyes were poking through the *New York Post*.

"Mr. Van Blunker," the turkey announced, "I have the honor to present Miss Maud Throckmorton. She seeks the nursing spot."

The old goat put down his paper and gazed up at Maud. "Come forward, my dear," he said in a voice brittle with age. "I don't see very well."

Maud crept closer.

"I presume, Miss Maud, that you're a nurse."

"I can nurse the worst," Maud parlayed with pride.

"Miss Maud," said Mr. Van Blunker, "I'm a fussy old goat who's not so ill. Mostly, I'm bored. I come from one of the old New York families, so I'm rich and do what I choose with desires that are many but meek. Mostly, I meddle in other people's lives. In that regard,

I expect you to regale us with a diary of your daily doings. Have you any objections so far?"

"No sir," said Maud, who would have agreed to anything.

"Good. Then we shall take you on. For the most part, your time will be your own. Feel free to roam the house. We have bundles of books on the second floor. Wilted tulips are in the garden. There is a ballroom on the third floor, where Evelina Telesforo and I occasionally waltz for old time's sake. On the roof is a pitcher's mound. I not only root for the New York Giants; in my youth, I used to pitch for the Downtown Dutchmen. What are your thoughts?"

"I'll take the job," said Maud, "though I'm not too big for baseball."

"You might consider it," said the old goat. "Baseball has provided me a lifetime of loyal friends. Why, in her days of glory, Evelina Telesforo was our catcher. Have you any curiosity that way at all?"

"None," said Maud.

"A pity," said the goat. "Still, I think we'll get on. Evelina Telesforo, show Miss Maud her room."

In a few moments, the turkey returned to the goat.

"The young rat is in her room," she said.

And the goat said, "Excellent. Please extend my compliments to our old teammate and friend Uriah Pilwick. Tell him that all has been rigged just as he requested."

Chapter the Eleventh
BIG DADDY DUDS MAKES HIS MOVE

NOT TOO LONG after Maud bolted, Bertha told Duds what had happened. The big rat was ripping mad. "The whole world does what I tells them," he shouted. "'Cept my daughter. Daughters are supposed to listen to their fathers!"

"She does listen," Bertha said while calmly chomping another chocolate. "She just don't like what she hears."

"What she don't like don't do donuts to me," yelled Duds. "We're moving uptown to Central Park."

Sure enough, that night—with a full moon in the sky to show the way—something like five hundred downtown rats, old and young, male and female, took off for Central Park.

Duds had his gang well organized. They came in squads of sixteen. Each squad was led by a lug—thirty-one lugs in all. For each five lugs there was a lieutenant. On top of the six lieutenants was Duds himself.

They all marched up Broadway. All the lugs lugged guns, which is why they got that name. Behind the gang came wagons full of furniture and clothing, plus gobs of baseball gear. Hired wharf rats did the heavy hauling.

Of course, while most of the rats walked, Duds, Bertha, and Pilwick sat in Duds's new Locomobile Steamer Car. A young lug took the wheel. Another walked alongside, a pistol in each paw.

Tossing along at ten miles an hour, Bertha held her large hat to her head. In the other paw, she held some peonies. The flowers came from Pilwick. Now and again, Bertha stuck the flowers to her eyes to hide her tears.

"Do you know where Maud went?" Duds asked his wife.

"No," she said, telling the truth.

"Don't matter," said Duds. "I'll find her." Then he turned to Pilwick, seated on his other side, and said, "Hey, Pilwick, youse know where Maud moved?"

"No," he lied.

"Well, find her. Quick."

"I'll try," said Pilwick, his possum face posting no passion.

Once the rat gang reached Fourteenth Street, they turned onto Fifth Avenue and continued uptown, even though it was a downtown street. At the Plaza at Fifty-ninth Street and Fifth Avenue, they entered Central Park through the Scholars' Gate. From there they went along Park Drive. Pretty soon they reached the Mall, spread out, and took up places near the Lake.

Duds celebrated the gang's coming to Central Park with a dance atop the terrace. The hired band consisted of a silly seal, a calico cat, a yellow yak, and a camou-flaged kangaroo. As the quartet rolled out ragtime tunes, the rats danced beneath the light of the immense May moon. Big Daddy Duds was parked inside the park and staying pat.

Chapter the Twelfth
OSCAR MAKES A DISCOVERY

AND OUR PAL Oscar? What was doing with him?

Now, it just so happened that the same time Big Daddy Duds and his rat gang were blowing into Bethesda Fountain Terrace, Oscar, straw boater on his head, was strolling through the park. What he was doing was his regular evening mayor's work: greeting friends and helping voters. Since things appeared mostly gravy, he tried to whistle up a tune—but his mouth wasn't wet.

See, though Oscar was trying to think about the park voters' needs, he was as upset as if Times Square had turned into Columbus Circle. The point being, Artemus Bigalow was still missing, and the regular Wednesday game had to be forfeited. And Oscar couldn't find nobody who knew where the cat was.

The worst part was that if the Central Park Green Sox didn't play the postponed Saturday game against the Wall Street Bulls, that too was going to be forfeited. And see, the Manhattan League had rough rules: Forfeit two games, and you were lobbed out of the league.

No wonder Oscar was as perky as a pancake without no cake.

In fact, Oscar, wanting to call up some calm, nipped over to Navy Hill. This here hill was a plot where he could take in the park and the Lake in peace. A self-soothing spot.

And it was a peachy night. The air was balmy. The high moon was busting big and beautiful. The Lake surface was soft as sluiced silk. Now and again, an owl hurled in with a helpful hoot.

"It's still great here," Oscar said.

But then, when he looked round toward Bethesda Fountain Terrace—what did he see? He saw a rat.

Oscar was surprised. Rats in Central Park were as rare as a city snowstorm in June. Just to see *one* rat made Oscar nervous. Oscar had read in the papers about rat gangs downtown. But not uptown. Not in Central Park. And rats had a rep for being bullies.

This particular rat was standing on the edge of Bethesda Fountain Terrace, staring out over the Lake. Oscar saw what looked like bright diamonds flashing on his paws.

Then the next minute, he spied a second rat.

Then a third.

And right near the rats was a possum.

"Twenty-three skidoo," Oscar said to himself. "What's going on here?"

He was still staring at the rats, trying to decide what he should do about them, when a sound came from behind him. He did what any self-respecting squirrel would do: He leaped for the nearest tree. Wasn't 'til he reached the safety of a big branch that he looked back around.

And what did he see? He saw another rat. This one was wearing a high-neck sweater, baggy pants, and hobnail boots. He also had on a baseball cap with the letter *B* on it.

But what Oscar noticed most of all was that around this rat's waist was a belt into which a pistol had been poked.

"Hey," said Oscar. "Who are you?"

And the rat said, "The name is Stuey, pal."

"Stuey?" Oscar said. "What are you doing here?"

"I'm guarding Big Daddy Duds's territory, that's what," said the rat. "And Duds don't like no strangers strolling soft. So, next time I see youse sneaking into the neighborhood, there ain't going to be no warnings. Just one less sappy squirrel. What's your name?"

Oscar blinked. "I'm Oscar Westerwit. The mayor of Central Park. Who is . . . Duds?"

"He's the rat that's just taken over this here parcel of park. So unless youse want to come down and mix it up, you better haul off."

"Haul off?" Oscar said, so slapped with surprise that all he could do was echo what he was hearing. "What did you say about this being . . . Duds's territory?" he asked. "And did you call me a . . . stranger?"

"Bet your busted britches I did," said the rat. "From now on, this here park is Rat Land. If I was you, squirrel, I'd skip, slide, and skedaddle out soon." The rat grinned, showing bright, white, and very sharp teeth.

"But . . . but, you can't just take over the park," said Oscar. "It's . . . a public place. Lots of folks live here: mice, chipmunks, voles, and squirrels. And besides, like I said, I'm the mayor here."

Before Oscar could finish his speech, Stuey pulled his pistol, pointed it right at Oscar's head, and winked the trigger. The bang popped a bullet that punched a pothole right through Oscar's hat of straw.

Oscar, frightened halfway out of his buttons, bolted so fast he all but flew over Bow Bridge. In fact, he didn't stop running 'til he was on the far side of the Lake, behind Warbler Rock. Then all he could do was stand and pant.

After a few moments, he took off his boater and looked at the hole the bullet had made. He even poked a finger through it before looking back across the Lake. The rat that had shot at him was marching up and down Navy Hill like a guard.

"This isn't even half right," said Oscar. "You can't just shoot mayors. Or anyone, for that matter." He looked back at the rat. "I better get the cops," he said. "They can deal with this."

Chapter the Thirteenth

OSCAR AND THE COP

Now, Central Park has all these entrances. At most of them, a square police kiosk had been built. These kiosks were small, tall, wooden boxes with pitched roofs and one open side, big enough to allow a cop to sit on a stool and keep watch—which they did, twenty-four hours a day, seven days a week. There was even a telephone for emergencies, plus an electric streetlamp to give some light.

So Oscar, holding his hat in his paws, came kicking up to the kiosk on Seventy-second Street and Fifth Avenue.

Soon as he saw a cop sitting there, he breathed better.

Only problem was, the cop, a big old bulldog, had his high-domed blue helmet tipped down over eyes that just happened to be closed. What's more, his paws were folded over his jacket with its double row of bright brass buttons; the buttons were so tight they looked as if they might turn into popcorn any moment.

Not that it mattered to Oscar. He ran up to the kiosk and gave it a rap. "Hey," he cried, "wake up. Cops are needed!"

The cop woke with a start, leaped up, and saluted. The thing is, when he saw only Oscar, he stopped and sat down again, eyes barely open. "Says who?" he said.

"Why, me," said Oscar. "And I'm the mayor of Central Park."

"According to who?" said the cop.

"Why, everyone."

The policeman gave a grunt, folded down a frown, and took pad and pencil from his pocket. After peeling over a few pages, he said, "What's your trouble?"

"Officer," said Oscar, "Central Park has been invaded."

"Who done the invading?

"Rats."

"Rats . . . invade . . . park," the policeman wrote on his pad.

Oscar went on. "A gang of them have taken over

the Bethesda Fountain Terrace area. Not only did I see them, I was bullied. Shot at. Look." He held up his boater where the bullet busted through.

The cop, hardly glancing at the hat, wrote: "Rat . . . shoots . . . squirrel."

"I was told," said Oscar, "that a Big Daddy Duds is the boss of these particular rats."

The policeman stopped writing. "Did you say . . . Duds?"

"That's what I was told."

"What's your name again?" asked the cop.

"Oscar Westerwit."

"What's your trade?"

"I told you. I'm the mayor of Central Park."

"You got proof about any of this, Westerwit?"

"Officer," said Oscar, "I just showed you my hat with the bullet hole, didn't I? Do you think I'd put it there myself?"

"And what, Westerwit," said the policeman, "was you doing wandering about Central Park in the middle of the night?"

"Officer," said Oscar, "I live here. I was out for a stroll. How many times do I have to tell you? That rat is right there on Navy Hill—with a gun. You've got to do something."

The policeman popped pad and pencil back into his pocket. From a small shelf he grabbed a thick, blue-bound book and began to finger his way through its

pages which, naturally, were dog-eared. "Got to check the rules," he said.

"Officer—"

"Rats . . . rats . . . ," the policeman said under his breath, touching paw to his wet tongue each time he turned a page. "Nope," he said, "nothing about rats."

"But I was attacked," cried Oscar. "Told to move away. Shot at! Called a stranger."

The cop set his reg book back on the shelf. "Listen here, Mr. So-called Mayor," he growled. "There ain't no rules about rats being in the park, with or without pistols."

"But . . ."

"As for Mr. Dudley Aloysius Throckmorton, he's a respectable citizen of the highest rep who's to be accorded all due consideration. I'm quoting Titus P. Snibly, the police commish. He's Duds's pal."

"*Pal?*" cried Oscar.

"You might better say best friends. So if you think the police want to heft your problems, get yourself another lifter. Or hoist them yourself."

With that, the policeman hauled down his hat, folded his paws across his chest, and closed his eyes.

"But Officer," Oscar shouted, "I'm the mayor of Central Park. I insist you do something!"

The cop peeked up from beneath his cap. "Listen here, Pal," he said, stabbing a stubby paw at Oscar, "you want to be arrested for disturbing the peace?"

"I want the law to act," said Oscar. "Are you deaf, dumb, or both?"

"One more insult from you," said the cop, "and I'll clap you in the clink for cussing. Now scram."

"*But . . .*"

"Get!"

Oscar turned away.

But as soon as the squirrel left, the cop lifted his telephone. "Officer Dupont Alphonse here," he said. "I need to speak to Police Commissioner Titus P. Snibly. On the double-quick. There's a touch of trouble."

Chapter the Fourteenth

THE NEW CENTRAL PARK

SO WHAT OSCAR did was bumble back through the park. "I don't believe it," he kept muttering to himself. "I don't. How can some rats just come in here and take over a part of the park? And that cop won't do anything. It's not the way things supposed to be."

Oscar let his feet guide him toward his rooms. All he wanted to do was sink into his easy chair and smooth out his hard thoughts. Trouble was, he was so bound up in brooding, he banged right into a barrier.

He looked up. A bunch of branches blocked the

path. Two rats were hanging over it. One of them had a pistol in his paw. The other had a rifle. On their faces—smirks.

"Hey," said Oscar. "What's this?"

"Borderline," said one of the rats.

And the second rat said, "Only rats allowed into Duds's domain."

"But . . . but I . . . *live* here," Oscar cried. "My rooms are right over there. In that elm tree."

"That the place with a big soft chair?" asked the first rat.

"And a nice big bed?" sneered the second.

"Sounds like my place," Oscar said.

"Bust your britches, buddy," said the first rat, shifting from smirk to grin. "We just moved in."

"So you better find yourself some other dump to doze," said the second rat. "In fact, if I was youse, I'd take yourself right out of this here park."

Not believing what his ears were hearing, Oscar could only stare at the rats—and their guns. Fact is, he was so speechless he couldn't speak. Eyes trickling with tears, he turned away.

And what did those rats do? They laughed.

Oscar worked along a path through the trees, trying to unscramble the hash in his head. A quarter of a mile on, he came on the Quigleys.

These Quigleys were chipmunks—father, mother,

plus four kids—who lived in the root cellar of Oscar's tree. Oscar liked them, had even taken the youngsters to ball games once in a while. And he—being a ballplayer plus mayor—was pretty much their hero.

But at the moment the Quigleys were hauling a two-wheeled wagon heaped high with household goods.

Now of course Oscar could pretty well guess what was happening: the rats. But since he didn't know what he could do about it, he decided to act the innocent.

"Well, well, the Quigleys," he cried out with his usual good cheer, "hope you're not moving. I'd hate to see you go. You've been good neighbors."

His high greeting was met by low looks.

"We have to go, Mr. Mayor," said Mr. Quigley, a plump fellow with gray about his ears and reading glasses gracing his nose. "They gave us no choice."

"'They'?" asked Oscar.

"Rats."

"Mr. Mayor," said Mrs. Quigley, "we were lucky to have gotten any of our possessions out at all."

"They said we were ugly," one of the youngsters added, kicking hard at a wagon wheel.

"You mean . . . the rats?" said Oscar, knowing he couldn't very well pretend he didn't know no more.

"Exactly, Mr. Mayor," said Mr. Quigley. "They appeared from nowhere, beat on our door, told us we had thirty minutes to move."

"Said I couldn't even take my bat," put in one of the youngsters.

"Or mine," said another.

"There were six of them," said Mrs. Quigley. "Three had cudgels. Two had guns. All had insults. Mr. Mayor, there are bands of them breaking into all the neighborhood houses. They didn't just evict *us*. It's everyone."

"Some families had no time to pack at all," added Mr. Quigley. "I suppose we were luckier than most."

"Mr. Mayor," said Mrs. Quigley, "do you know where they came from?"

"Downtown."

"But . . . why have they even done this?" she asked.

"Not sure," said Oscar. "But they're led by someone named Duds. I suspect he's copped the cops."

"Heavens to betsy and beyond," cried Mrs. Quigley.

"But you're the mayor," said Mr. Quigley. "Can't you do something about it?"

All Oscar could say was "I'm working on it."

"I should hope so," said Mrs. Quigley.

"My dear," said Mr. Quigley to his wife, "we really have to go."

With that, the chipmunks grabbed their wagon bars and began to pull. The youngsters pushed from behind.

"Loads of luck!" Oscar called after them.

But even as he stood there, another group, this time the Billhops—a squirrel clan—came pounding down the path. They didn't look at Oscar, and he didn't have the heart to heave no words. He was pretty sure what happened.

In fact, before the hour had halved, seven more park families pounded by. All of 'em had been evicted from their homes by rats.

"But . . . this is Central Park," Oscar kept saying to himself. "This ain't supposed to happen here."

Except, see, it had.

Chapter the Fifteenth

WHAT OSCAR SAW

So OSCAR, WHO was pretty well dunked into a dull daze, went wandering about under the light of that big full moon. As he ambled about, he kept talking to himself: "Just how many rats have invaded the park? Where they going to stay? What are they going to do? What am I supposed to do? I'm mayor. Shouldn't I be doing something? But what?"

Oscar hiked 'til it was almost dawn. Frustrated as a floppy fish in a frying pan, he decided to climb to the top of Warbler Rock. From there, he hoped, he could *spy* over to Bethesda Fountain Terrace and learn something more about the rats.

Sure enough, when he reached the rock top, he could see the Angel of Waters fountain clear and easy in the early morning light. What's more, he saw the sculptured cherubs around the base. These baby angels were known as Purity, Health, Peace, and Temperance.

Just seeing them got Oscar so stirred up he slapped a paw over his heart and wept big weepers. After all, Purity, Health, Peace, and Temperance were exactly what all true New Yorkers—like him—believed in! Trusted! Lived by!

But then, when Oscar took a gander beyond the upper terrace, his heart tattooed. 'Cause what he saw there was gobs of rats. And they were having a dance. He could hear the music. It wasn't even what he liked. It wasn't even Broadway show tunes, either.

The scene filled Oscar with so much rage that he made a fist, shook it, and shouted, "Down with rats!"

Which is when this voice called from right below: "Oscar, dear boy, what are you doing up there?"

Oscar looked down. And who do you think was calling him? His mother, that's who.

Oscar's mother—her full moniker was Hilda Pennypacker Westerwit—was a widow who liked to wear billowy skirts and black silk blouses to hide the fact that she was pretty itty. Except, on her head, she always wore a huge, wide-brimmed hat with paper flowers and real feathers. In one paw, she had a parasol. In the other paw was a pokey little purse of polished jet. Her tail was thin with age, and all in all she was fairly fragile. Except for her voice. That was more the bull-moose type.

"Now that you're mayor, Oscar," she called up, "I never know what you're doing, do I?"

"Ma," said Oscar, "I think you better come up here and take a look."

"I can't imagine what's left for someone my age to see," said Mrs. Westerwit. "But if you say it's interesting, dear boy, I can only hope it's something worth a gossip."

So up she climbed.

"All right, then," she said when she got to the top, "which way shall I look?"

"Over there." Oscar pointed across the Lake.

Mrs. Westerwit took her eyeglasses from her purse, set them on her nose, and peered over to where Oscar was pointing.

"Why . . . great goodness and gum galoshes," she exclaimed. "There seems to be some kind of . . . party. Well, I had *no* idea. I certainly was not informed. Or invited. Oscar, dear boy, have I been left out? Whose party is it?"

"Rats'," said Oscar.

"Rats in Central Park?" said Mrs. Westerwit, her voice building like a flight of steps. "Giving a fancy dance party? On the terrace? The most fashionable place in the park?" By the time she had done, she was just about shrieking.

"It's true, Ma."

"Oscar," said his mother, "how could you ever let such a thing happen?"

"*Me?*"

"You *are* the mayor, are you not?"

Oscar told her what he knew—which wasn't very much.

Mrs. Westerwit said, "Well, then, I suppose the rats are not entirely your fault. But still, what do you intend to do about them?"

"Ma," said Oscar, "you can see for yourself how many there are. And they've all got guns."

"Don't you think you should go to the police? I'm sure the authorities would chase them away."

"I did go," said Oscar.

"Then when will the rapscallions be peeled away?"

"Ma," said Oscar, "I was told that unless I stopped telling the cops to do something, they'd put *me* in jail."

Mrs. Westerwit drew herself to her full half height. "Oscar," she said, "I am not amused."

"That's what I was told, Ma."

Mrs. Westerwit put away her eyeglasses. "Well, then, dear boy," she said, "that means you'll have to take on these ruffians yourself."

"Why me?" said Oscar again.

"Surely being mayor of Central Park means something besides parties, singing, and dancing. It's time to put aside silly baseball games and take care of serious business. Really, Oscar, it's only what's expected."

"But Ma . . ."

"I'm depending on you," said Mrs. Westerwit, giving her son a quick kiss on his cheek. "Indeed, I'm sure the whole park is depending upon you. Now—will you still be coming for breakfast this Sunday?"

"Ma," said Oscar, "when was the last time you were home?"

"Why, earlier this evening. I was visiting with poor Mr. Van Blunker, who has just hired—"

"Ma," Oscar interrupted, "the rats may have taken over your apartment."

Mrs. Westerwit turned a pasty pale. "My home? Taken over? Surely, Oscar, I would have thought that by now you would have learned that I really have no sense of humor."

"Still, it might be true."

"Oscar," his mother said in a trembling voice, "I need to go and see."

With that Mrs. Westerwit skidded down the rock and rumbled off so fast Oscar had to rocket to catch up.

Chapter the Sixteenth

DUDS IN CENTRAL PARK

WHILE THIS WAS going on, what was Big Daddy Duds doing?

Well, right cross the Lake from where Oscar and his mother had just been spying, Duds was sitting soft and sassy in his new office under the steps that led from the terrace to the Mall. That way he could look out the windows at the angel fountain and the Lake—which, far as he was concerned, now belonged to him.

Leaning back in his big leather chair, which was behind an oak desk, he was listening to the party music and puffing away on a cigar like a pig iron factory.

"Pilwick," he said, "this ain't too half bad."

The old possum, who had a smaller desk to one side of the room, was touching up the account books. "Yeah, Boss," he said, without looking up from under his derby.

"I likes this place a lot," said Duds. "In fact, I like it so much I've already started asking myself if maybe we should take over the rest of the park. We could charge admissions. Make us another pile."

"Whatever you say, Boss."

"I did say," said Duds. He leaned back, sucked some smoke, and thought for a while. He took a long look at the possum and said, "Hey, Pilwick, what's with Maud?"

"Don't know."

"You still looking for her, ain't you?"

"Sure thing, Boss."

"But you ain't found her yet, is that right?"

"Nope."

Duds looked sour pickles at the possum. "This ain't like you, Pilwick. Just understand: I'm figuring on you to find her. And if things don't add up, I'll have to do my own subtracting."

"Sure, Boss," said Pilwick as he bent over his books.

Duds was about to say something else when one of his lieutenants came into the room. "Hey, Boss, a couple of guys want to see you."

"Yeah, who?" said Duds.

"First is one of our own lugs named Stuey. The other is a reptile. Wouldn't give his name."

"Is he green?"

"Yeah."

Duds grinned. "Sure thing," he said. "Tell this Stuey to come on in first. When he goes, I'll speak to the other."

"Okay, Boss."

Duds laid out some paper and pens on his desk to make it look like he was busy. "Take care of your own first," he said. "You do understan' what I'm sayin' about Maud, Pilwick, don't you?"

"Yeah, Boss," said the possum.

So, who should come in but Stuey, the rat who took a pothole shot at Oscar on Navy Hill. He stood all nervous before Duds's desk.

Duds leaned back in his chair, looked up, and said, "Okay, Stuey, what's on your brain?"

"Boss," said Stuey, "I need to tell you about this here squirrel."

"Give you trouble?"

"Some lip."

"With squirrels," said Duds, "if it ain't lip, it's tail. What's his name?"

"Goes by the name of Oscar Westerwit. Says he's the mayor of Central Park."

"Mayor, huh? I hope you voted him out," said Duds as he wrote down Oscar's name on a bit of paper.

"I tried, Boss. Only I missed."

"Hey, don't worry. I'll take care of him. Now get back to your post and keep your eyes to the open."

"Okay, Boss." The rat headed for the door.

"The only thing, Stuey," Duds called out. "If that there squirrel shows his nose again, make sure you nick him good. In my league you only gets one strike."

"Yeah, Boss," said a frightened Stuey as he went off.

"Okay," said Duds, "get the reptile in here."

Pilwick stood up.

"Hold it," said Duds. "Put some cash in an envelope and let me have it."

The possum did as he was told, then brought in a short, squat, green lizard dressed in a dark suit. His collar was high and starched. His beady eyes were constantly blinking and his tongue kept going in and out.

"Hey," said Duds, "it's Titus P. Snibly himself! New York's police commish!" He shook the guy's thin paw—with its small but sharp claws—as if he were pumping a well for water.

"Hey, Duds," said Snibly, "it's a pleasure seeing you again."

"The joy's jumping all over me, too, Pal," said Duds. "Haul in a seat."

"Don't mind if I do," the commissioner said, taking a chair opposite Duds.

"Are our Brooklyn Superbas doing okay or what?"

said Duds with a grin. "Did they beat Cinci and Philly or what?"

"They did."

"Okay. Enough tiny talk. What do you need?" Duds said. "Cigar? Glass of champagne? Maybe a bottle of champagne?"

"Mr. Duds," said the commissioner, "I only just learned that you and your family moved into the park. I wanted to be the first to welcome you uptown."

"We appreciates it. We really does."

"Will you be staying long?" the commissioner asked.

"Could be," said Duds. "So far, I'm enjoying myself. The fresh air. The trees. They ain't too bad."

"How much of the park are you going to use?"

"To tell the truth, Snibly, I'm not too sure. See how it goes. And how's by you? Everything doing okay?"

"Everything is fine," the commissioner said with a thin smile, his tongue whipping in and out. "But of course, that's what I get paid for."

Duds grinned and pitched the envelope cross his desk. "Here's a little fancy to freshen your feelings."

Not looking, the commissioner popped the envelope into his pocket and stood up. "I do want to warn you about one thing," he said. "There are many old families around the park. They don't always take to newcomers."

"Snooty, eh?" said Duds. "Don't worry nothing about us. We'll dish them a daily dose of Duds." He shook hands with the commissioner again. "Hey," he said, leading the guy to the door, "you ever hear of a squirrel goes by the name of Oscar Westerwit?"

"Westerwit," said the commissioner. "He comes from one of the city's oldest squirrel families. Around the park they call him mayor."

"A real mayor?"

"No."

"Got any clout?"

"He's a better ballplayer than a mayor, which is not saying very much."

"Great," said Duds. "I love losers I can lick."

Soon as the commissioner left, Duds sat himself down behind his desk. He picked up the paper with Oscar's name on it. "Hey, Pilwick, you need to scout about this here squirrel, this Oscar Westerwit. See what kind of a mayor he is."

"He's manager and shortstop for the Central Park Green Sox," said the possum. "Artemus Bigalow was his pitcher."

"How'd you know all that so quick?"

"It's my job to know what to know when it's worth the knowing."

"Then find out about Maud. Do we understan' me, Pilwick?"

"Whatever you say, Boss," said Pilwick.

"I did say," said Duds.

Chapter the Seventeenth

MAUD MAKES A DECISION

Now while Daddy Duds was showing Snibly the door, what was happening to Maud?

If you can remember, she was in the top-floor room in Van Blunker's fancy Fifth Avenue pile. She had unpacked, but it didn't take long to put what little she had away.

So there she was, sitting on the narrow bed, not sure what she was supposed to do. Should she go down to the old goat? Should she wait until she was called? She knew she could always read her medical book—but she was in no mood for that.

The fact is, though she'd found a job and a place to

live, she wasn't leaving to the larks. She was still angry about Artemus Bigalow. She was still angry at herself for loving him. She was still angry at her father for sending the cat away. She wished, in fact, she had done so herself.

So what she did was wander through the house, trying to avoid the goat and the turkey.

First she visited the library on the second floor, but the books were only about goats. Then she looked in at the tulip garden. Except the flowers were folded and the leaves were limp. She found it depressing. She peeked into the third-floor ballroom, but it was empty.

Finally, she went up to the roof to look at the pitcher's mound. With no one there and feeling full of frustration, she flicked a few sizzling strikes, including Bigalow's big knuckleball-spitball special. But since it was the cat that had taught her to throw, she quit in disgust.

Still feeling bad, she rolled back to her room and peeked out the window. It was nearly dawn. Central Park was all in green and flowers. Though there were storm clouds winking in from the west, she liked what she saw. She'd been so busy running away from home, she'd never really noticed the park when she came. Now that she saw it, she was glad to have the park close. In fact, she was thinking that maybe what she needed was a quiet life when there was a knock on the door.

It was Evelina Telesforo.

"Mr. Van Blunker presents his compliments," said the turkey, "and has asked me to inform you that he has no need for you for the rest of the day. He looks forward to the pleasure of your company for dinner, served promptly at six.

"He further suggests you take a stroll in the park. There is a nearby social establishment at The Rocks called The Rock and Mole Café. Park inhabitants often congregate there. You might make friends."

With that, Evelina Telesforo bobbed a few times and strutted away.

Maud agreed: A walk about the park might be the best thing for her. And maybe, she thought, she'd even visit that café.

Chapter the Eighteenth

OSCAR'S MA'S HOME

BACK TO OSCAR.

Now you might recall that Oscar's ma, Mrs. Hilda Westerwit, was stomping through the park like a hook and ladder galloping to a five-alarmer. "Those rats wouldn't hurt my rooms. . . . They couldn't," she kept muttering as she marched along. "It wouldn't be right. It wouldn't."

"Ma," said Oscar, breathing hard to keep close, "you need to lower the speed and raise the caution."

But Mrs. Westerwit plunged on.

When Oscar finally caught up to his old lady, she

had reached a stand of trees, an antique grove near her apartment.

"Ma," Oscar kept pleading, "those rats don't fool around. You could get yourself hurt."

"The idea," his mother said, "of getting hurt by going back to your own home. Absurd!"

"I just want to make sure everything is okay," Oscar said, trying to calm her. "Then you can go."

"Oscar, if I wanted drama in my life, I'd go to the theater. You go to Broadway plays all the time. Did you ever see anything such as . . . this?"

"I only go to musicals, Ma."

"Very smart of you, I'm sure. Too much realism is quite unrealistic!"

"I won't be long," said Oscar. "Just promise you won't go anywhere."

"How could I? There's no place to go."

So Oscar handed off his hat to his mother to hold, then hurried through the trees.

When he got to the Lake, he pulled off his jacket, socks, and shoes, rolled up his trousers over his knobby knees, and waded into the water. Moving slow, he worked his way through the tall grass, making sure his tail was above water but not too high, not wanting to give himself away.

Pretty soon he heard a harsh, raspy sound. It started, then stopped, then started again.

A puzzled Oscar kept going.

When he got to the end of the grass, he spread some aside and looked out. What he saw was the nearby shore as well as the trees that made up his mother's neighborhood. But what he also saw was six rats standing round his ma's tree. The tree, one of the oldest in the park, looked over the Lake and an island just beyond.

Four of the rats had pistols and rifles. Two more were working on the oak tree's trunk with a bucksaw, pulling it back and forth. What they were doing was cutting down his ma's home.

Shocked and shaken, Oscar stared as the two rats working the saw stopped. They stepped away, only to be replaced by two other rats, who kept the saw sliding.

It was all Oscar could do not to crash in on the party. What stopped him was knowing he couldn't stop them. The moment he lifted his nose, he knew the rats would plug him.

Sure enough, one of the rats standing on guard shouted, "There's one!"

Oscar ducked. But it wasn't to him the rats were pointin', but over to some low bushes. In fact, there was a frantic rustle right at that spot. Whoever was hiding must have known he'd been peeked. Two of the rats lifted their guns and begin blasting away. Next second, there was a high-pitched squeal, and . . . silence.

Oscar held his breath.

"Good shot," said one of the rats. "The shout of it is, he ain't got long."

Oscar, heart pounding like a locomotive hauling uphill, kept staring into the bushes, trying to see who'd been hit. He was hoping whoever it was had got away.

As for the rats, they went back to cutting down the tree.

And Oscar—though feeling pretty frantic—couldn't keep from watching.

"There she goes!" one of the rats shouted.

With an enormous CRACK, the old tree went toppling toward the water. There was snapping and crackling—like popcorn popping—as branches broke. Dirt and leaves flew. Water plumed. The rats cheered.

No sooner did the tree come to a stop than the rats started bopping off big branches. They scrambled over the trunk, shovels in hand, using the tree as a bridge to the island.

As Oscar watched, they began to dig on the island, putting up walls.

Suddenly Oscar got what they were doing: They were building a fort, a fort that could command the Lake. If they did that, they could take over the entire park.

Chapter the Nineteenth

UNCLE WILKIE

OSCAR, FLUSTERED FROM his feet to his forepaws, hurried back to where his ma was waiting, nervous and jumpy.

"Dear boy," she said soon as she saw him, "what's happened? I heard an enormous crash. Have you any idea what it was? Is it all right to return to my apartment?"

"Ma," said Oscar, "you don't have a apartment anymore. The rats cut it down. They turned your boudoir into a bridge."

Mrs. Westerwit fainted.

It took time for Oscar to get his old lady up. Even so, there were tons of tears and temper.

"Ma," said Oscar, "I think you're going to have to move in with Uncle Wilkie."

"I don't like him," said Mrs. Westerwit. "My brother-in-law thinks only of himself. Never of me."

"But I don't know of any other place you can go," said Oscar.

"If I must," she said.

So they set off across the park.

Now Uncle Wilkie Westerwit was a stout, squat, older squirrel gent who used to be a lawyer. He didn't win a lot of cases, but that was okay with him as long as his clients paid his rent. They must have done so, because he became rich. Then he lost most of his dough investing in Colorado gold mines that broke out bust. So he retired, raked his garden, and wrote his memoirs. He had already filled two thousand, six hundred, and forty-two pages and he had yet to be born.

When Oscar told him about the rat invasion, Uncle Wilkie humphed and said, "In my day this would not have happened." Still—though he only had a couple of rooms—he was willing to take in his sister-in-law.

But after putting Mrs. Westerwit to bed with some chamomile tea to nurse her nerves, Uncle Wilkie took Oscar aside.

"Nephew," he said, "something must be done about these rats."

"Sure, Uncle," said Oscar. "But what?"

"Have you considered suing them?"

"Uncle, they aren't going to care. They're thugs. Besides, it would take years. I'm not wanting to court the courts."

"All right, then," said the old lawyer. "If you can't sue, make a deal. That's the way to get on in the world. You're the mayor. It's what a mayor is supposed to do."

"What kind of deal you talking about?"

"These rats may be bad. But if you're nice to them, you'll see, they'll come to depend on us. We squirrels are better bred. Deep inside, rats know it. That's probably why they came. They want us to like them. Just make sure you separate us from the others in the park—the mice, chipmunks, and rabbits. I won't even mention the birds. All perfectly pleasant in their fashion, but flighty. In the end, Oscar, we squirrels have to look out for ourselves."

Oscar shook his head. "That kind of deal isn't my dodge, Uncle. Anyway, like I said, these rats are thugs."

"The bigger the thug, the bigger the deal," returned Uncle Wilkie.

"I don't think I can do it," said Oscar.

"Oscar," his uncle said, "as mayor, you *must* do something."

"Uncle Wilkie, there are lots of them and all with guns."

"Nephew," said Uncle Wilkie, "you're a Westerwit. There's family honor to consider."

"You don't understand, Uncle. These rats almost killed me. I saw them wound—or maybe kill—someone else. Lots of good voters have been driven off. Friends of mine. There's nothing to deal."

"Oscar, a shrewd deal maker always deals himself a dish for dinner."

Oscar shook his head.

"All right, then," said Uncle Wilkie, "I'll have to manage things my way."

"What's that supposed to mean?"

"You do things your way," said Uncle Wilkie. "I'll do things mine."

Oscar, too weary to argue, took himself away.

Chapter the Twentieth

THE STORM

OSCAR, FEELING so low the grass seemed high, trudged slowly cross the park. Not knowing where to go, he just kept moving. Any time he caught a glimpse of someone—didn't matter who—he shied off. He was too tired to keep explaining he couldn't do anything about the rats. It was too painful. Better to be alone.

Besides, the morning sky was full of rolling gray clouds. Trees were swaying. Birds were swirling. Flowers were rocking like waves. A storm was coming on.

Oscar remembered Sam's words of just a few days ago. "You know what?" his rabbit pal had told him. "You're a romantic."

Though the thought made Oscar sigh, he tried to sing:

"O dry those tears, and calm those fears,
Life is not made for sorrow;
'Twill come, alas!
But soon 'twill pass . . ."

The words faded fast.

Instead, he slipped into some soft-shoe steps. Took maybe four figures. The pedi-patter petered out.

"Romantic!" he snorted. "Me? I'm a failure. Useless. Can't even protect my beloved park. My home. Or anybody else's, for that matter. I'm supposed to be the mayor of Central Park. But there's nothing I can do."

Feeling like the bottommost brick of the biggest New York building, Oscar bumbled about the Ramble. Skirted Azalea Pond. Tripped past Tupelo Meadow. Came back toward Balanced Rock.

Lightning started licking overhead. Thunder came next. Rain started to fall. Wasn't long before it poured.

Oscar scampered up a tree and sat below a leafy branch. Once there he squatted down, drew up his tail, and clapped his boater on his bean. Rain ran through the bullet hole and nibbled down his nose.

"Central Park is great," he muttered beneath his breath. "At least it was great. No more."

Then he remembered something else Sam had said: that he belonged in a Broadway show. Or a musical, anyway.

So as Oscar sat there—moist and miserable—he tried to think how things would work out in a show. Didn't take long to plot: He'd fight back, win himself a sweetheart, and live happily ever after.

Oscar shook his head. He'd settle for a single scene: the one in which he'd sock each and every rat in the snout.

But then, see, as Oscar started thinking about it, if there really was such a fight, there couldn't be much doubt about the outcome. After all—he thought—didn't justice have to triumph? Didn't good *always* win?

Sure as sunlight.

Just having the thought brought Oscar back some boost.

Didn't take more than a minute more before he told himself that since the rats were no good, maybe the only way to show the thugs a thing or two was by . . . greater force.

So Oscar started trying to think up ways of fighting the rats. He figured, considering how many there were, it would take lots to defeat them. In fact, as he saw it, it would take an . . . army.

A large army.

Oscar decided that if park voters really understood how bad the rats were, they'd *have* to enlist in an army—right on the spot.

In other words—as Oscar saw it—soon there'd be a pretty army, pretty large and pretty fast.

He'd call it the Army of Central Park. Naturally, he would be the general. After all, he was the mayor. He'd be another George Washington. A Grant. A Teddy Roosevelt.

Oscar told himself that once he had his army, he'd need to work out a plan of attack. That shouldn't be too hard. In school he'd read about some battles. Surprise attacks seemed to work. Catch the enemy unawares. That way he'd be . . . victorious!

Oscar's heart began to burn like a barn fire.

Hey, since the rats were up to no good, they had to be . . . cowards! Of course they were. Bullies and hooligans were always inside cowards. When attacked, they probably wouldn't even fight back. They'd just go back from where they came—downtown.

Sitting in the tree, Oscar could actually see the rats beaten to bits and begging to get away.

"Hurrah!" Oscar shouted right out loud.

He tried to stay calm. There were some things to work

out. Instance: Should his army have uniforms? Blue ones. Or should they be green? The right uniforms—Oscar thought with growing excitement—would look great at the banquet.

What banquet?

Why, the banquet that celebrated the victory over the rats. You *had* to have a banquet when you won. That's when he'd give up being general of the army and return to being just mayor and, yes—playing baseball.

But that banquet would be perfect for giving his farewell address. It'd have to be a great speech. Brilliant. Good enough to put in history books. So kids would read it. Memorize it. Take tests on it.

"Fellow voters of Central Park!" Oscar shouted. "We, who have just beaten our foes, we, who have restored justice and tranquility to Central Park, we must thank all them who joined up with an equal degree of justice, modesty, and—"

That's when Oscar heard a moan.

Chapter the Twenty-first

THE MOAN

OSCAR STOPPED HIS speech on the spot and searched around.

Nothing.

But when the moan came again, he figured it had to be coming from a clump of flowering azalea bushes not far from the tree he was in. He looked at the spot hard. For all he knew, a rat was going to bean him with a bullet.

But when the moan moaned a third time and no shot sizzled, Oscar crawled out of the tree and worked his way over to the bushes. He shoved aside some leaves, and what did he see? It was his good pal Sam, the right fielder for the Central Park Green Sox. The rabbit was laid out like a welcome mat without much welcome left.

Sam's clothing was cut. His face was filthy. His ears limp. One of his lucky paws was pressed against a bloody shoulder.

"Hey, Sam," said Oscar, "it's me."

"Oscar?" said Sam, his voice as weak as a fish out of water.

Oscar knelt down by his pal's side. "Sam," he said, "what happened?"

"Rats," said Sam. "I was over to your old lady's place trying to find you. Hiding in the bushes, see, wanting to stop them from cutting down her tree. Only they seen me first and tried to kill me second."

Oscar, realizing it was Sam he'd watched the rats bop before, only asked, "How bad is it?"

"Real bad."

"Your throwing arm?"

"The other."

"Then you'll be okay," said Oscar. "But I better get you home," he said. "Fetch a doc."

Sam gave his ears a feeble shake. "Hey, Pal. I don't got no home. The rats ripped it."

"You can't stay here," said Oscar. "You need something over your head. Can you walk if you lean on me?"

"I'll try," said Sam.

Oscar helped his friend up. While the rain rumbled, the two sloshed through puddles while Oscar kept an eye for shelter. Trouble was, the rain came so chunky Oscar couldn't see too good.

Worse, Sam started to shiver. His breathing became brief. "Oscar," he groaned, "I don't have much health."

Oscar stopped and looked around. Through the rain, he could only make out a jumble of boulders. Still, it was the most likely place for getting out from the wet.

"Just a little more," Oscar said.

"Can't . . . go . . . too far," the rabbit whispered.

Oscar, all but carrying his friend, pushed on. When he saw a gap between two rocks, he aimed for it. Trouble was, it looked only wide enough to squeeze through on a wheeze.

"Wait here," said Oscar. He lowered his friend to the ground and squirmed into the hole. It led into a dim, musty cave. Only a little rain had leaked in, which made it a whole lot drier than outside. Oscar went back for Sam.

Crawling inside turned all the rabbit's get-up-and-go into lie-down-and-stop. He stretched out limp and soggy.

"I'm going to get some help," Oscar said, and rushed off.

Out in the rain again, Oscar looked around. This time he saw where he was. Lick-split, he tore over to the other side of the rocks and came to a door that had a sign nailed over it:

THE ROCK AND MOLE CAFÉ

Oscar dove in.

Inside the café were a couple of mice, some starlings, and a pigeon. They were in working clothes, except one of the mice who was in a suit and derby. A few squirrels were sitting round a table playing cards. Other squirrels at another table were talking baseball. A chipmunk couple was cuddling close and whispering cute. On the stools before the counter were two more chipmunks talking with Molly, the bar mole, as she polished the counter with a cloth.

And over in a far corner, who should be reading a book? It was Maud.

Now, when Oscar ran into the room, everyone looked round. Maud too peeked up from her book. And what did she see: Oscar looking wet and wild. His whiskers were frizzled. His tail looked like an iron rope. His grimy, green baseball duds was drooling pools of water onto the floor like a big green sponge.

But Maud, she found him interesting.

"Hey, Oscar," called one of the card-playing squirrels, "how about a song?"

"No time for songs!" cried Oscar. "I've got an emergency! Sam's hurt bad. He's been shot."

So, of course, as you might have also guessed, Maud stood up. "I'm a nurse," she said. "Can I help?"

"You sure can," said Oscar, barely looking at her. "Follow me. He's around the corner."

"Show me where."

Oscar wended his way back to the cave. Sam was lying on the ground, still as sawdust. Maud knelt by his side and plucked his pulse.

"What do you think?" said Oscar.

"He's pretty weak. What happened?" she asked.

"Shot by rats."

Maud looked around. "What do you mean?"

Oscar told her what happened.

Maud listened hard. And though the squirrel didn't mention Duds, Maud, who was no dummy, could dope the doings for herself. Not that she said anything. All she did was turn back to Sam.

"Go back to the café," she told Oscar. "I need hot water and clean cloth."

"Sure thing," said Oscar, and he busted back to the café.

"Hey, Oscar, is Sam all right?" Molly asked soon as he got back through the door.

"We need hot water and clean cloth," said Oscar.

"Coming up!" said the mole.

A jug of hot water was fetched, along with some

clean towels. Oscar took them up and started back.

"Hey, Oscar," one of the chipmunks called. "Ain't youse going to tell us what's happened?"

"Nobody move," Oscar yelled. "I'll be right back."

So Oscar beat it back to the cave and gave Maud what she wanted. And here's the thing of it: It was only when she took the stuff that Oscar suddenly said to himself, *Hey, this doll is a rat.*

Maud, who wasn't paying much attention to Oscar, just to Sam, said, "Prop him up on you. I'll work on his shoulder."

The two of them rigged the rabbit up 'til he was leaning against Oscar. When Maud peeled away Sam's torn jacket, he groaned.

"He going to be okay?" Oscar asked.

"You got to him halfway to the nick," said Maud.

Oscar watched her work. "What's your name?" he asked.

"Shhh," she said. "I'm working."

Maud washed Sam's wound and bound it, then covered it with clean cloth. "Ease him down," she said. "He needs to rest."

Oscar did what Maud told him.

Pretty soon, Sam, breathing easier, dropped off to sleep.

"Now what?" said Oscar.

"You better go back to the café and clean yourself up," said Maud.

"What about you?"

"I'll sit with him 'til you get back. I'm not going any-where 'til dinner."

Oscar held back. There was something about this Maud that made him think he'd rather stay.

Only she said, "You better go."

Oscar started to head off, but stopped to thank Maud. And the thing of it was, when he looked at her, he had this thought: *Hey, this is one beautiful rat.* Not that he said anything, except, "Thanks. I bet you saved my pal's life."

"We both did," Maud said with a sudden smile.

Oscar took that smile in like it was sweet summer sunshine sauce. "Now . . . can I ask your name?"

"Maud."

"Maud. I like the name," said Oscar. "My name is Oscar. Be back as fast as I can." With that, he tore himself away.

Chapter the Twenty-second

OSCAR MAKES AN ARMY

So Oscar hauled himself back to the café.

"How's your friend doing?" Molly asked from behind the counter.

"Better," said Oscar. Only thing was, by that time, Oscar wasn't thinking so much about Sam as he was musing about Maud.

"Hey, Oscar," asked a squirrel, "what's going on?"

"Soon as I get my breath," said Oscar, stepping up to the counter. Actually, he was trying to get Maud off his mind. I mean, considering what was going on, it didn't seem too right.

"How about a drink?" Molly said.

"Some wet water," said Oscar.

The mole brought the drink in a tumbler.

Oscar downed a dab, then leaned back, elbows resting on the countertop, hind foot hooked on the foot bar.

Everyone was silent, waiting for him to say something.

Hey, he was thinking, *this is just like I was some actor in some play.*

"Does anyone," he finally said, sort of slow-like, "know what happened?"

The silence took another plunge.

Oscar whisked down another wash of water and then said, "A gang of rats has run over Bethesda Fountain Terrace."

"They did?" said one of the chipmunks.

"They came in last night, Chester," said Oscar. "Haven't come for a social call, either. Or a stroll. They've taken over a hefty piece of park. Homes. Territory. There's been abuses. Attempted murder. Theft. That's why Sam was shot. It's an invasion. I think they're trying to take over the whole park."

"The *whole* park?"

"Sure looks that way to me."

"That really true?" said one of the mice.

And Oscar, nice and easy, said, "Anyone ever hear of a rat named Big Daddy Duds?"

"He runs a rat gang downtown," Molly piped in.

"Maybe he used to be downtown," said Oscar. "But now he's right here in Central Park. With a load of friends."

They all stared at Oscar.

That's when Molly said, "These folks have been working all night. They've only just dropped in on their way home. Don't know much."

Oscar nodded. "So none of you guys have gone back to your homes yet, right?"

"Just been here," one of the starlings said.

Talking nice and easy, Oscar said, "Hate to inform you, Harry, but when you get back home, you might find an unhappy bolt from the blue. There's a good chance your place has been busted in or turned out."

Next second, one of the squirrels threw down his cards, jumped up, and raced out of the room. Then one of the pigeons popped out.

"They've got big families," Molly explained.

"How many of these rats . . . are there?" asked one of the chipmunks.

"Loads, Thad," said Oscar. "And they're armed tooth to tail. One of them put a bullet through my boater. Like I said, Sam was shot. Some others cut down my ma's tree, one of the oldest oaks in town."

"Cut down a *tree*?" a number of voices sang out.

"I saw 'em do it," said Oscar.

"But that's . . . illegal."

"Cowardly."

"Not nice."

"Maybe. But that's what they're doing," said Oscar.

"But . . . but Oscar, you're the mayor," said a chipmunk. "What you going to do about it?"

"Glad you asked," said Oscar, stepping away from the counter and taking up a place in the center of the café. "What I'm going to do is, toss those rats right out of the park."

"How you going to do that?"

"I'm going to put together an army."

"An army!"

"You mean," said one of the mice, "you intend to have a . . . war on them rats?"

Oscar stood there, feeling the limelight. "Fellow voters," he cried, "if there's to be any justice in the park, the good must fight the bad. These rats are cowards. Who else would sneak into the park in the middle of the night and just take over and have a dance?

"Are we going to put up with that? No! Are we going to stand up for our rights? Yes! Do you want to be known as stay-at-homes? No! Do you want to free the park from punks and march to victory? Yes!" By this time Oscar was shouting out his words. In fact, it was all he could do to keep from dancing.

"Who's going to do the leading?" someone called out.

"I will," Oscar cried. "What's more, I'll do it if I have to fight alone. But I'd feel a whole lot better if some of you voters joined in. How about it? Who's going to fight those rats with me?"

The silence blew up big. No one looked at nobody else.

It was a mouse who finally lifted a paw. "If I can be useful," he said, "I'll . . . join."

"I guess . . . I can too," said a chipmunk.

"Can you use me?" a starling joined in.

"Woodrow, we can use everyone!" Oscar shouted.

One of the squirrels at the card table rose up. "I'll join," he said. He looked around. "The sooner we drive out the rats, the better."

Oscar leaped to the countertop. Not able to help himself, he did a quick tap step. "Fellow Central Park voters," he cried, "this is a day to remember. We're going to protect our liberties and our trees. Fast, too. From here on in our motto is"—he thought furiously—"One blow and out they go!"

There was a burst of cheers as everyone jumped up. There were even more cheers when Molly said, "Drinks are on the house."

The excitement didn't stop there. The animals pressed around Oscar, asking questions about what they needed to do.

Thinking fast, Oscar told them that the first army drill would take place the next night on Cedar Hill fields. It was an open space, far from the terrace and

Mall where the rats were. The moon—he figured—would still be big and bright.

"The sooner we attack, the better," Oscar let everybody know. "We don't want those rats to settle in too deep."

"Are you sure we'll win?" asked a chipmunk.

"Win? Why, I intend to maul them in a New York minute," said Oscar. "After all, we're right. They're wrong. True, the bigger the army we have, the faster we'll win and send them back downtown."

There were lots more cheers.

"Every voter needs to enlist," Oscar shouted over the din.

"What about weapons?" one of the birds asked excitedly. "You going to supply them?"

"Bring what you got at home."

"And if you don't have any?" one of the squirrels wanted to know.

"Bring what you got," Oscar said, and shook paws with them all. "Remember. Cedar Hill. Tomorrow night. First drill. "'One blow and out they go!'"

Everyone—save Oscar and Molly—raced on out.

Oscar stood there, exhausted.

It was Molly who said, "Oscar, you put on quite a show. All we needed was music."

Chapter the Twenty-third

DUDS HAS A VISITOR

Now, LIKE I told you when I started off, this story has loads of loops. So here comes one of the big ones.

Big Daddy Duds was in his terrace office, sitting behind his big desk. His lieutenants—including old possum Pilwick—were gathered around.

"I like this here Central Park," Duds was saying. "I like the green. Reminds me of money."

"Yeah, Boss," said one of the rats. "The whole gang likes it."

"Good. Because what I've decided is, I'm going to take more."

"We started building a fort on the Lake," said one of the rats.

"I like that," said Duds. "I like that a lot."

"Only thing," said the rat, "I had to shoot someone hiding in the bushes. He was spying on us."

"Good," said Duds. "Anyone else have problems?"

"I chased a whole family out of their house," said one of the rats, grinning. "They moved pretty fast when they sees we were serious."

The others laughed.

"I hunted out a few myself," said another.

"Me too."

"Hey, you guys done great," said Duds. "But it ain't over 'til the rooster lays an egg. Someone's bound to get the idea of doing something to get back at us."

"Not this bunch, Boss."

"Don't be so sure," said Duds. "All I knows is that in the gang business the minute you go easy, they come back hard. Just when you think they're stupid, they'll throw smart at you. Think they're weak, someone pops you strong in the snoot and, trust me, it'll hurt.

"So, 'til I tell you otherwise, I want guards posted round our territory twenty-four hours a day. I want drilling once a day. Now, get on with it. And come up with a plan for taking the rest. Remember, I like easy, but I'm willing to hit what's hard."

The rats shuffled out of the room. Only Pilwick stayed behind.

"You really going to take over the rest of the park?" the possum asked.

"Pilwick, it's like I told them, if I can find an easy way, I will. Hey, speak of finding, you find Maud yet?" Duds asked.

"No."

Duds gave the possum a pointed eye. "Pilwick, I'm not so happy with you. Usually you come up with fat answers. How come you're so thin on this one?"

"She's smart."

"True. She's my daughter. So I'll give you a few more days. Understan' me?"

"Sure."

"Anything else?" asked Duds.

"There's a squirrel here who wants to see you. An old one."

"A squirrel?" said Duds. "Squirrels are suckers. Show him in."

The thing is, the guy who walked in, dressed in his best suit, white gloves, and gray spats, was none other than Oscar's Uncle Wilkie himself. In one paw he even held a gold-capped cane.

"Mr. Throckmorton," said Uncle Wilkie. "It's a great pleasure to meet you."

"Likewise," said Duds, giving the squirrel a suspicious study. "Grab yourself a seat."

Uncle Wilkie sat. "Mr. Throckmorton—"

"My friends call me Duds."

"Mr. Duds . . ."

"Just Duds."

"Well then . . . Duds," said Uncle Wilkie, "I've been impressed with the speed and efficiency by which you have taken over such a large section of Central Park."

"Is that so?" said Duds.

"You remind me of Napoleon. Of Ulysses Simpson Grant."

"Yeah, I heard of them guys."

"We park squirrels can offer nothing but admiration."

"You telling me you're glad we're here?" said Duds, trying to square the old squirrel.

"I won't lie to you," said Uncle Wilkie. "It's not a question of being pleased. Would I rather you had left us alone? Of course. But here you are, so I think we must accept it." He smiled.

"Yeah," said Duds. "You get yourself two runs for that one."

"Indeed," Uncle Wilkie went on, "we squirrels might as well cooperate and be helpful to you. Both squirrels and rats could be better off."

Duds studied the squirrel. "What about the rest of the voters?"

Uncle Wilkie offered another thin smile. "I'm sure they can take care of themselves. After all, rats and squirrels, we are both rodents."

"Hey, Pal," said Duds, "what you after here?"

"All squirrels want," said Uncle Wilkie, "is peace and order."

"What did you say your name was?"

"My friends call me Uncle Wilkie."

Duds leaned back in his chair. "Okay, Unc. Let's see if you really mean what you're mouthing."

Uncle Wilkie managed another smile.

"Here's the deal," said Duds. "You keep your eyes and your ears unplugged. Know what I'm saying? Find out what's wiggling. If someone's working against me, you roll right on over here. Understan'? Give me news I can use and I'll give you some decent views. We done a deal?"

"I think so," said Uncle Wilkie.

After Uncle Wilkie left, Duds settled back in his chair. "Hey, Pilwick," he said, "what you make of that?"

"I'm not sure."

"I'm not so sure neither," said Duds. "But you know what? Maybe we have ourselves a spy."

And Duds gave himself a smile.

Chapter the Twenty-fourth

OSCAR TALKS

BACK TO OSCAR.

After starting to put together his army, Oscar left the café. The rain had stopped. The air was sweet. Birds were flying. Even the sun was sunning. Oscar was excited as a bag of popcorn popping. It wasn't just the army. What he kept seeing in his mind was a picture of Maud. Which he liked.

So what he did was go back into the cave.

He snuck in quietly, so at first Maud didn't know he was there. And what hit his eyes? The nurse was sitting by the side of the sleeping rabbit. But the thing of it was, all Oscar could see was just how much peaches and cream this particular rat was.

Then Maud heard him, looked around, and smiled.

The smile set Oscar's heart to slamming. Still, all he said was, "How's Sam?"

"He's doing okay," said Maud. "And you?"

"Fine, thanks," he said. "I have to say, you've done a good job. I bet you're tired."

"I'm used to it," said Maud. "I'm a nurse."

"Bet you're a good one."

After which said, there was this slice of silence that slipped between them—sort of like a wall that wasn't there—but which was there, if you know what I'm saying.

Finally Oscar said, "You live near here?"

"Not too far."

"In the park?"

"Not really."

"What were you doing in that café?"

The questions started to make Maud feel uncomfortable. She shrugged. "Just there."

As for Oscar, he had never felt so tied tight in the tongue. "You might like to know," he said, "while I was in the café, I made an army."

A look of alarm ran up Maud's face. "An army?"

"I've got lots of voters joining up. There'll be more, too."

"What," asked Maud nervously, "you going to do with an . . . army?"

"Oh," said Oscar, like it was no major moment, "we're going to chase the rats away. Present company excepted, of course," he tossed in.

Maud thought about that for a moment, swallowed hard, and then said, "Ain't you scared?" She was looking Oscar right in the face.

"Not really. We'll win. No doubt about it."

"How come?"

"Because we're right."

Maud turned away and fussed with Sam's bandage. "Is that what you want? Having a war?" she said. It was as if she were dancing on a high wire that might go slack any moment.

"To tell the truth," said Oscar, "since I'm the mayor, I should be out helping voters. I'd be doing that now, if these rats hadn't invaded. The boss rat seems to be named Duds. I'd like to meet him and give him a piece of my mind. He needs to be told what's right."

"And . . . do you think that'll be easy?" Maud said, her voice on the squishy side.

"Hey, the way I see it," Oscar rolled on, "this Duds is nothing but bunk and bluster. A coward to boot. But what can you expect? He's in the wrong."

"Who's going to be in charge of this army of yours?" Maud asked faintly.

"Me," said Oscar. "We'll start drilling soon. Hey, we might even need a nurse. Want to be a part?"

Maud, feeling full of fumbles, kept her eyes on Sam.

"I'm not so sure your friend should stay here" was all she said. "He should be in a bed. Some decent food, too. Where's his home?"

"The rats took it."

"I can't take him to where I'm living," Maud said. "Could he stay in the café? I could look in once and a while."

"Sounds good to me. I'll go and ask," said Oscar. "Or maybe you want to? You could use a break."

Maud thought for a moment. "Sam's your friend. You should do it."

"Be right back," said Oscar. "Just wait here." And off he ran.

So Oscar went back to the café. Molly was behind the counter. This time she was washing glasses.

"Everything okay?" the mole asked when Oscar appeared.

"Better and better," said Oscar. "But we need to find a place for Sam to stay. His home was taken over by the rats."

"I've got a back room," said Molly. "With a bed. He's welcome here."

"Thanks. We'll get him there."

"I'll have things ready," said Molly.

Oscar hurried back to the cave. Sam was there, still asleep. But the thing of it was, Maud was missing.

Chapter the Twenty-fifth
MORE TALK FROM OSCAR

NOW THOUGH OSCAR was puzzled and upset that Maud had sailed, he still needed to get Sam to the café. So he dropped to his knees beside his pal. "Sam," he said.

The rabbit opened his peepers.

"It's me, Oscar. Got to get you up and move you to a better place. Think you can do that with me, Pal?"

"I'll try."

Oscar helped the rabbit to his lucky feet. With Sam leaning on him, they made their way to the café. Molly came out from around the counter to help. They guided Sam into a small back room, a storage place with only candlelight. Against one wall was a cot on which they laid Sam.

"You okay?" Molly asked the rabbit.

Sam nodded. Then he said, "Hey, I had me a dream."

"What was it?" said Oscar.

"I dreamed this beautiful rat was my nurse. Ain't that wild?"

"That's just perfect, Pal," said Oscar. "Now try to get some rest."

"And I'm right outside the door," said Molly. "Call if you want anything."

"I will," said Sam, and he shut his eyes.

Oscar followed Molly back into the main room.

"Lucky that nurse was around," Molly said as she stepped back behind the counter.

Oscar said, "Who is she?"

Molly turned to polish the counter. "She came in this morning, took a corner seat, started to read."

"Do you think . . . she could have been one of . . . *them*?"

"The invaders? Sure didn't act it."

Oscar said, "Just now, when I went back to where I'd left her—with Sam—she'd gone."

"How about that," said Molly.

"The thing is," said Oscar, "I told her about the army. I'm wondering if she might toss the beans to the other rats."

"Let's hope not," said Molly. "You better get some sleep," she suggested. "Have a place to stay?"

"I can bunk with my uncle up by the Ramble. But I'll be back and check on Sam. Thanks for your help."

"Don't worry nothing about your pal," said Molly. "And good luck with your army. Let me know if I can help."

So Oscar frisked his feet toward his uncle's house. As he padded through the park, he kept alert for rats and tried to keep his thoughts on matters military. But the fact is, what was really ragging in his mind was Maud. What if she was a spy and riled the rats about his soldiers? He kept hoping she wasn't. He wanted to see her again. Then it occurred to him that Molly hadn't really answered his questions about Maud. Got him wondering what the old mole might see in that direction.

Anyway, all that was meandering through his mind when Oscar got to his Uncle Wilkie's house. His mother was sitting in the front room, having tea.

"There you are, dear boy," she said. "Have you fixed everything? Are the rats gone yet?"

"Won't be long," Oscar told her. "Where's Uncle Wilkie?"

"He had to see someone. I expect him back soon."

Oscar dropped into a chair.

"Now tell me what you've been doing about those

dreadful rats," said Mrs. Westerwit. "I've always hated them. Even before this happened. They are all—each and every one of them—quite awful."

Oscar squirmed. "Maybe not all," he said.

"Oscar," said Mrs. Westerwit, "there's no need to be fair about it. It's perfectly fine to be fair when you're on top. But when you've been treated badly, fairness is surely not to be favored."

"Well I don't know—," began Oscar, only to be cut off by the arrival of Uncle Wilkie.

"Just in time for tea, brother-in-law," said Mrs. Westerwit. "We must all carry on as foolishly as before. It will demoralize the enemy."

Uncle Wilkie took off his white gloves and set aside his gold cane. "Ah, Oscar, my boy, have you been out and about, busy defending the park?"

Oscar said, "I've set up an army."

"An army!" his mother cried. "How exciting."

"It is indeed," said Uncle Wilkie as he drew up a chair. "I do so want to hear all about it."

So, since Oscar decided it wouldn't be so merry to talk about Maud, instead, he told them all about his army and what he planned to do.

And guess what? Uncle Wilkie had lots of questions.

Chapter the Twenty-sixth

MAUD AGAIN

Now, if you've been tagging after this tale all this time, you probably want to know why Maud took off.

See, Oscar's words about war rolled her into one rattled rat. What she did was trot on back to the Fifth Avenue mansion. Evelina Telesforo opened the door.

"Ah, there you are," said the turkey. "Just in time for dinner. Mr. Van Blunker is waiting at the table."

The welcome flustered Maud even more. She was in no mood to munch, though she knew dipping into dinner was part of her job. So she followed the turkey.

The dining room was big with candlelit chandeliers

dangling from the ceiling. The table was long but set only for three. The china was fine, and there was more silver than in a Nevada mine. Napkins were big as bedsheets. As for the food, it was boiled cabbage and butterscotch pudding.

The old goat, Mr. Van Blunker, dressed in a tux and tie, was at the head of the table.

"And how are you getting on, Miss Maud?" he asked when the rat took her place.

"Pretty good, thanks," said Maud.

The goat exchanged a look with the turkey. "Is everything to your satisfaction?" he asked.

"Sure," she said, though the fact is, she felt like crying.

"I should remind you," said the goat as Evelina Telesforo served Maud a plate crowded with cabbage, "that one of your responsibilities is to tell me what you do each day. Being a shut-in, it's nice to know what's out in the world."

Which is when Maud turned to tears.

Mr. Van Blunker and Evelina Telesforo exchanged gapes.

"Miss Maud," said the goat, "you must share your sadness."

Maud stared at her plate as if it were a mirror. She was trying to decide if she should say anything. Could she trust them or not?

Unable to decide, she bolted from the table and ran up to her room.

Upstairs in her room, she stood by the window, staring out. "Maybe," she said, "it'd be better if I just went away."

She sat down on her bed and made herself think of what she really wanted to do. "To take care of Sam," she heard herself saying.

But the next moment came another question: *What about Oscar?*

And this time the thought came: *I'd sort of . . . like to see him again.*

Chapter the Twenty-seventh
OSCAR'S ARMY

EARLY NEXT MORNING, Oscar went rushing around the park—wherever he could go—trying to yank in more recruits for his army of the park.

"We're going to win," he told anyone willing to listen. "We're going to win because right is on our side. And what's right always rules."

Problem was, not too many voters signed up. True, a whole lot had already been chased away—homes taken or destroyed by the rats. Most of those folks didn't think they had a minnow's chance in a sea of whales to wash the invaders out. But there were others who just didn't want to join an army. Some were scared. Or lazy. Or had better things to do. So, by late afternoon, Oscar was still trying to seek more soldiers.

Now, the thing of it was, all the time Oscar went about his recruiting, he couldn't keep Maud out of his mind. For instance, he wondered where she lived. If he would ever see her again. If he *should* see her again. After all, his cause would be in tons of trouble if she turned spy and dipped to Duds about the army he was doing.

Even so, as Oscar kept trying to top up his troops, he found himself creeping closer to The Rock and Mole Café. So, sure enough, when he found himself all but next door, he decided he needed to visit his pal Sam. Besides—this is what he told himself—there was the possibility of doing some recruiting at the café.

As usual, Molly was behind the counter polishing glasses. Seemed like polishing was what she mostly did. As for patrons, there were none save a single gent in a corner. He had his head resting on the table and was sound asleep, snoring.

"Hello, Molly," Oscar called.

"Hey, Mr. Mayor," said Molly. "How's it doing?"

Oscar took a quick look around—saw that Maud wasn't there—and was embarrassed he even had the thought. But all he said was, "I'm fine. How's Sam?"

"Much better," said Molly. "He got a lot of sleep, and when I last checked, he was sitting up. That nurse was here a couple of times, too."

"She was?" Oscar said, in his best soapy-soft voice—though his heart drummed out a *tat-tat-rat*.

"Said she'd look in one more time, tonight. But go on in and say hello."

Oscar went into the back room. Sam was sitting up, shoulder newly bandaged, soaking up a copy of *The Baseball Weekly*.

"Hey, Pal," said Oscar, as he came in.

"Hey, Oscar!" Sam cried. "Good to see youse."

"Can't give up on my right fielder," said Oscar. "You doing all right?"

"Much better. And thanks for getting me that peachy nurse."

"Oh? She been around?" Oscar said, acting surprised.

"Sure has. She was asking about youse, too."

"Like what?"

"You know, where youse come from? What do youse do? That kind of stuff. She knows oodles about you now."

"How come?"

"I told her," said Sam.

All of a sudden Oscar, sitting there, was wishing he didn't have to put the army together. "What did you learn about her?" he said.

142

"Didn't ask," said Sam. "What's been going on?"

They talked some more, but Oscar was not talking what he was thinking. In fact, he was so rattled and restless he said, "I've got to go organize the troops. What time did you say that nurse was coming back?"

"She didn't say exactly. Late."

Oscar, promising he'd come back after the drills were done, left the café.

Chapter the Twenty-eighth

THE ARMY OF CENTRAL PARK

Now CEDAR HILL fields is in the north part of the park, which was pretty far from where the rats had settled in around the terrace. And since it was the month of May, there was still plenty of light for early evening.

Oscar hurried over to the place, wanting to be on the field first so as to greet his army and start the training. He knew he was supposed to bring a gun—at least that's what he had told the folks at the café to do. Thing was, he didn't have one. So he was hoping that others could find and bring some firepower. The rats, he knew, had plenty.

Trouble was, what he found at the field was just fifteen voters. The moment Oscar saw them, his heart sank below sea level. Not only were they a bedraggled bunch, they were looking as mean as marshmallows, and melted marshmallows at that. They had dressed as best they could, which meant they were all different colors and sizes, no two looking alike. As for firepower, one squirrel did have an old Civil War musket. The rest, if they had anything, brought sticks, brooms. Sure, one of his Green Sox teammates, the mouse Engelbert Maxamillion, brought a baseball bat, but a baseball bat wasn't going to do much for a major battle.

Two others from the team that also came were Thaddeus Twilliger and Cyrus X. Furdly. Oscar made them sergeants. But to Oscar's eyes, his troops were more like a bad chorus line in a third-rate vaudeville show than an army. And though he tried hard not to be discouraged, he couldn't help hoping that heaps more would be joining in. "There's work to do," he told himself.

Taking a deep breath (and trying to be cheerful), he cried, "Fall in, Pals!"

The fifteen would-be soldiers stood shoulder to shoulder. They looked like the jagged New York skyline at dusk—as seen from Jersey.

"Soldier voters," Oscar cried, hoping he growled like General Grant. "I like your faith in justice. You're a fine contrast to the rats' meanness. Where we'll bring bravery to the field, they're nothing but cowards. Most of all, we believe in our cause and ourselves! And for all those reasons, we can't lose!"

The troops applauded politely.

And sure, a few more voters crawled in, until, all in all, Oscar's army numbered thirty. Maybe, he kept telling himself, they'll turn ferocious. Maybe the rats would be cowed. Numbers—he told himself—didn't have to matter. At least that's what he was trying to believe himself.

Anyway, he marched his tattered troops up and down, trying to teach them that when he shouted "To the right, march!" they would go in that general direction.

And the truth of it was, they *did* get better. Oscar had them hang together as they heeled to the right and left, and sometimes straight. They presented arms—such as they had, aimed in the right direction, and pretty much did what he told them.

He began to feel better and told himself, "Maybe we got something here."

Once the drills were done, Oscar gathered the troops together again. Even before he could speak, one of the squirrels asked, "When do we attack?"

"Tomorrow, I guess," said Oscar.

"What time?"

"Midnight," Oscar said, choosing the most dramatic time. "We'll meet here first."

Having said that, he watched as his army faded away.

Oscar, alone, sighed. "Tomorrow I've got a war. Tonight I better go see Sam," he said, though you can be sure he was thinking more of Maud.

Anyway, when he got to The Rock and Mole Café, there were only a few voters there.

Oscar told himself he should give his recruitment speech to get more soldiers. But before he could speak, Molly called, "Hey, Oscar. Sam's doing better. And that nurse is with him now."

Quick as a quack, Oscar forgot about his army. Instead, he bolted into the back. There was Sam, propped up against a pillow, eyes bright, ears perky. And by his side was Maud.

She turned and saw Oscar. And when he saw her, Oscar's heart beat faster than the front drummer of a boys' Main Street marching band on Memorial Day. But all he said was, "Good evening, Miss Maud. How you doing, Sam?"

"Just great," the rabbit said.

"He's doing much better," said Maud, turning back to the rabbit so she could escape Oscar's eyes.

"What you been doing?" Sam asked Oscar.

Now Oscar was just about to tell him all about his army when he reminded himself that Maud might just be a spy. So all he said was, "Nothing much."

"Have the rats gone?" asked Sam.

"Not yet," said Oscar.

"Anyone playing ball?"

"Things are still too mixed-up. By the time you're better, we'll be playing again."

"Any word about Bigalow?" said Sam.

That name—Bigalow—made Maud look round fast. "Who is . . . Bigalow?" she said, kind of gargly.

Oscar said, "He used to be our star pitcher."

"What . . . happened to him?"

"Disappeared. No one knows why or where."

Maud blushed right up to her ears. "No idea?"

"Naw," said Sam, "the cat just went."

"Who's your pitcher now?" asked Maud.

"No one," said Oscar.

"Do you think . . . he'll ever show up again?" said Maud.

Oscar shrugged. "Nothing is the way it was," he said, which reminded him how edgy he was. "I better go.

"Nice to see you again," he said to Maud, and bolted from the room.

"That's funny," said Sam.

"What's funny?" said Maud.

"Most times Oscar is all talk."

Maud didn't say nothing. She was glad she was meeting her mother at the opera that night.

As for Oscar, he went out to the main room and leaned over the counter, his face full of forlorn.

"What's the matter?" asked Molly.

"I've fallen in love," muttered Oscar.

"Who's the lucky pumpkin?"

"The nurse," Oscar whispered, and he tore out of the café.

Soon as he went, Molly reached behind the counter, picked up a telephone, and asked for a number.

When she heard a reply, she said, "This Evelina Telesforo? Molly. Over to the café. Pass it on. Oscar has fallen in love with Maud. Sure, anytime." And she hung up.

As for Oscar, he headed for his Uncle Wilkie's house. All the way there, he kept asking himself if he'd been a fool for not talking more to Maud, or a fool for not talking less to a rat. At the same time, he was trying real hard to keep his mind on his army. "I've got a battle to fight tomorrow," he kept telling himself. "I don't have the heart for more heart."

By the time he reached his Uncle Wilkie's house, he'd made a vow that the only thing he'd think and talk about was the war against the rats.

His mother and uncle were in the front room.

"Dear boy," said his mother, "where have you been?"

"Organizing my army," said Oscar.

"Ah, your army!" cried Uncle Wilkie with bright eyes. "Do tell me all about it."

Oscar, glad to be talking about anything but Maud, told them how he was going to move against the rats.

"How utterly fascinating," said an eager Uncle Wilkie. "Just exactly when will you be doing that?"

"Tomorrow night. A surprise attack," said Oscar, and he sorted out all his secret plans to his mother and uncle.

And once Oscar told them all there was to tell, he fell sound asleep in a big chair. He was sleeping so deep, he didn't hear his Uncle Wilkie walk out.

Chapter the Twenty-ninth

MAUD AND UNCLE WILKIE

SOON AFTER OSCAR left the café, Maud excused herself from Sam.

Truth was, she was feeling full of fuzzy. The only thing she was certain of was that this particular squirrel, this Oscar Westerwit, didn't have no interest in her. She wished she could say the same about him.

She took a trolley downtown to the opera house, where she waited impatiently for her mother. The moment she saw her, she said, "Ma, I've fallen in love."

"Does that mean Bigalow is back?"

"It's a squirrel named Oscar Westerwit. He's the mayor of Central Park."

"Central Park! That's where your father took us," said Bertha.

"I know," Maud said sadly.

"In case you also wanted to know," said Bertha, "Duds told me he's getting ready to take over the whole park."

"I know that, too," said Maud. "And the one he's mostly wanting to chase out is the one I love."

"Baby, you ain't so lucky in your loves."

"Ma, I don't know what to do."

"We'll talk more during the intermission," said Bertha. "You go find our seats. I'll be there soon."

Soon as Maud went, Bertha wrote a quick note to Pilwick the possum. Next she found an usher and said, "I need to send this as a telegram."

The same night that Maud told her mother *her* news, Uncle Wilkie had gone off to see Big Daddy Duds in his office behind the Bethesda Fountain.

When he got there, he told Duds everything that Oscar had told him—that an army had been raised and was going to make a surprise attack the next night at midnight.

"Now that I've told you," said Uncle Wilkie when he had done, "may I remind you of your promise to treat all squirrels kindly."

"Don't worry nothing about it," said Duds. "We're going to treat them terrific."

"I'm delighted to hear it," said Uncle Wilkie as he left.

As soon as Uncle Wilkie went, Duds turned to Pilwick, who was reading a telegram he had just received.

"Pilwick," said Duds, "I like this. I like this very much. Call all our lieutenants. We need to get organized. Set up. This mayor of Central Park thinks they got a surprise for us. Well. We're going to snap a surprise for him."

Then, seeing that Pilwick was reading, he asked, "Hey, is that telegram for me?"

"Nothing I can't handle," the possum said.

Chapter the Thirtieth

READY FOR THE BATTLE

Now, Oscar, he kept telling himself his army was a lot better than it looked. He also kept thinking that soon as the rats caught a whiff of him and his warriors, they would turn their tails and trot on back to downtown.

So, Oscar was going to stick with his attack plan—the one he'd told Uncle Wilkie about the night before.

At the same time, Oscar couldn't move Maud out of his mind. So it was just about twilight—not more than a few hours before the big battle was to begin—that once again he rolled over to The Rock and Mole Café.

"Hey, Oscar," Molly called when he popped in. Like always, she was polishing something. "How you doing?"

First thing Oscar did was look around, you know, making sure no one would hear what he was going to say. There was no one, saving Molly, and some gent reading a paper. But the paper was so big Oscar couldn't see who was behind it.

Anyway, Oscar came up to the counter. "Tonight's the night," he whispered.

"The night for what?"

"My army is going to mash them rats at midnight. Poke them right out of the park."

"Got it all together then?"

"It'll be like plucking a daisy out of the dew," said Oscar.

"That a song or your strategy?" asked Molly.

"It's my strategy."

"How big is this here army you got?" asked Molly, pausing her polishing for a bit.

"Big enough," Oscar said, not exactly looking at the mole's eyes, which were never open anyway.

"Good luck," said Molly.

"Hey," said Oscar. "We'll take all the help we can get. How's Sam doing?"

"Better and better. In fact, that nurse is in there with him right now."

"She is?" said Oscar, tumbling all thoughts about the night's battle.

"Sure thing."

"Be right back," said Oscar, and he tore out to the back room.

The minute he went, Molly turned toward the customer reading the newspaper.

"Did you get all that?" she asked.

The newspaper lowered. And guess who was behind it? Pilwick himself.

"Sure did," the old possum said, standing up. "And that was Oscar Westerwit, right?"

"The mayor of Central Park hisself."

"Yeah. I seen him once before. Now just don't tell Maud I was here."

"Don't worry, I won't."

"Thanks, teammate," said Pilwick, and he padded out.

In the back room, meanwhile, Oscar saw a pretty smiley Sam, with Maud sitting by his side.

"Hey, Sam," Oscar said.

"Hey, Oscar," returned the rabbit.

As for Maud, all Oscar did was turn to her and say, sort of quiet-like, "How do you do, Miss Maud."

"Good evening," she said back, with not much more excitement.

The truth was, Oscar was so flustered he blurted out, "Hey, Sam, you're missing a big night."

"What's happening?" said Sam.

Right off, Oscar knew he'd made a mistake. He was telling himself: *What if this rat really is a spy?*

"Nothing," he sort of sputtered. "It's just . . . a nice night. I mean, the moon is bright."

So sure, they talked about a few things—mostly not much and the much didn't have much weight. Though he was dying to, Oscar didn't even hardly say a soft word to Maud. Fact is, he was even afraid to look at her.

As for Maud, she had her lips locked too.

It became so bad, just sitting around, that Oscar couldn't stand it. "Gotta go," he said. "Be back tomorrow in a better mood."

And out he ran.

Next minute Molly came into the room. "Hey, your pal just flew out of here. What you guys say to him?"

Sam said, "Nobody said much of anything."

"He must be distracted," said Molly.

"With what?" asked Sam.

"Didn't he tell you?" said the mole. "He's got himself an army. They're going to attack the rats tonight at midnight."

Maud grew pale. "*Tonight?*" she said.

"That's what he told me," said Molly.

So what did Maud do? She ran out.

"Hey," said Sam, "how come everyone is running away from me?"

Chapter the Thirty-first

MAUD

NEVER MIND OSCAR. Exactly where was Maud going, anyway?

She had decided to run away. She was going to gather her stuff and just go. Someplace. Anyplace. As long as it wasn't Central Park.

Okay, so she beat it on back to the old goat's Fifth Avenue pile. When she got there, she pounded on the door.

Evelina Telesforo opened it.

The turkey had a surprised look on her face, which,

let me tell you, being a turkey, ain't easy. "My dear Miss Maud," she said, "you told us you were out for the evening."

"I have to tell Mr. Van Blunker I'm quitting this job!" Maud cried, and ripped right round the turkey.

Evelina Telesforo trotted hard after her. "But Miss Maud, please! You mustn't just go there!"

Only Maud, paying no mind, burst right into Van Blunker's parlor. And who's sitting there on the couch, right next to the old goat? Nobody else but old possum Pilwick himself, that's who.

Maud stopped short like she had just run into a tall wall.

As for Pilwick, he peeked a look up at her through his thick glasses, but being on the shy side, his look didn't go too far.

Mr. Van Blunker allowed himself a cough and a pull on his chin whiskers. "Miss Maud, I thought you were to be gone for a while," he said. "But now that you have returned, there's much to say. I believe you know Mr. Pilwick. He's an old friend of mine. We once were teammates on the Downtown Dutchmen. And, I might add, we are both New York Giants fans."

Pilwick squeezed out a shy smile and dipped his derby to Maud.

"Mr. Pilwick," the goat continued, "is here to prevent a calamity."

"What kind of clams you talking about?" Maud found a faint voice to say.

"You are aware, are you not, that your father has come to the park?"

Maud nodded.

"And that he intends to take it completely over."

Maud nodded again.

"We have also learned," said Mr. Van Blunker, "that a war is about to break out. Blood will flow. Lives will be lost. We are trying to prevent that."

"But how—"

"Miss Maud," said Pilwick, "I think you have an acquaintance, a squirrel who goes by the name of Oscar Westerwit."

"How did you know that?" Maud muttered, blending in a blush.

Pilwick said, "It's my job to know what to know when it's worth the knowing. I also know that this here Mr. Westerwit has himself an uncle. Uncle Wilkie."

"That I wouldn't know," said Maud.

"He does. And this here Uncle Wilkie knows all about your friend raising up an army. What's more, he came and told Duds about the attack."

"If my father knew what Oscar was doing," said Maud, "he'd kill him. I know he would. Look what he done to Bigalow."

"The thing is, Miss Maud," Pilwick went on, "Duds not only knows what's what, and who's who, he also knows when's when. And your father can count noses as well as jewels. So he's got his lugs and lieutenants on the ready. He's going to put them park voters down."

"But what can we do?" cried Maud.

"There you are, Miss Maud," said Mr. Van Blunker. "That's just why my old teammate Pilwick came. He's got a plan. It's not an easy one. But it surely is a plan."

"It all depends," said Pilwick, "on what happens at the battle tonight."

Chapter the Thirty-second
THE BIG BATTLE

So THERE IT was. The moon might have been high in the sky as it moved to midnight, but Oscar's mood was hugging his ankles. His army had maybe thirty-six Central Park voters: squirrels, rabbits, a few mice, a couple of possums, maybe some chipmunks (including Thaddeus Twilliger), and a stray mutt or two like Parker Baladoni. Even some of them who done some drilling before had ducked. As for firepower, they had a bunch of brooms, a few baseball bats (the guys from the team), plus some odd sticks. Regarding guns, someone got his old man's Civil War gun, but he couldn't find no bullets.

Oscar, looking them over, kept telling himself they were better than they looked. Still, he was wondering if he shouldn't wink the whole war off. The trouble was, he had got this far and didn't know how to slip in a stopper.

But though his stomach was sloshing, Oscar gave another patriotic speech that was more bathos than bellicose.

"Gentlemen," he said, "there is no way we can lose. We're going to come onto the rats like firecracker fury. Soon as we do, the rats will heave their gats and go away. All we need to do is grab what they drop and keep on rolling until we get back the terrace. After that, we'll have a party. With music. Remember," Oscar shouted, "we can't lose!"

The thing of it was, his army believed him.

But by then it was time to tip on forward. The Army of Central Park—with Commander-in-chief Oscar Westerwit, hiz honor hisself, up front—came crawling down from the north side of the park, out along the east side of the Lake. They went through the Glade. They skirted round the Boat House on the Lake before turning east up the road. Then they headed right for Bethesda Fountain Terrace. The point being, it was there that Oscar thought the rats would be so sound asleep he could shake them by surprise.

Then Bethesda Fountain Terrace came into view. Only thing was, when Oscar took a peek over toward the terrace, what did he see? Right across their path,

blocking their way, a whole rank of rats. A major mess of them. Lined up. *Waiting.*

"Halt!" said Oscar.

His army stopped, bumping into each other. Busting one another's bunions.

Not wanting to believe what he was seeing, Oscar stared at the terrace. No double doubt about it, there stood a line of maybe one hundred and fifty rats on the ready, standing by in regular rows. What's more, each and every one had a gun.

"Is that them?" a skeptical squirrel asked Oscar.

The mayor of Central Park didn't answer. He couldn't. He was too shocked. Sunk. Staggered. All he could do was stare.

The rats were expecting them. His army was about to be slaughtered. Dumped into deep disaster.

"Mr. Mayor," one of his troopers whispered, "they don't look like they're really ready to run."

In fact, the rats had hefted their guns and pointed the heat right at the park army.

"Run!" yelled Oscar.

Oscar's army leveled out like a lump of ice on a midtown August pavement.

That's when the rats fired.

Oscar's army ran so fast—pumping feet faster than fury—it was like they were chasing hundred-dollar bills down a spring squall. They were heaving their brooms, sticks, and bats away like so many half-baked beans.

Yes, sir, they were going so many different directions a compass couldn't find them. Truth is, in one half of one half minute there *was* no army of the park.

And Oscar? He stood there like a tasty target with bullets bouncing by, up, down, and beside him. Then, before they could get inside him, he ran too, ran so hard he almost got in front of himself.

It was only when he reached the far side of the Lake that he stopped. He was alone, breathless. He was busted big. A total flop. All that had been lovely had been lost.

Chapter the Thirty-third

HIZ HONOR THE MAYOR AND MAUD

NOW IT TOOK time for Oscar to stop peering at the pavement, peel open his eyes, and point his snoot around. That was when he realized he wasn't too far from The Rock and Mole Café. Not knowing where else to go, or what else to do, he dragged himself there. So he walked in and who did he see? Maud, that's who.

All they did was look at each other. But, hey, sometimes silence speaks a lot smarter than speech. Except Oscar, ashamed, slumped down into a chair by a table and buried his head in his arms so deep it would have taken a steam shovel to pry him out.

Maud waited a minute. Then she slid over, drew up a seat, and sat by his side. "What happened?" she asked, soft as Coney Island cotton candy.

"We lost," said Oscar.

"Was anyone hurt?"

"Wasn't time for anyone to get hurt," Oscar said. "They knew we were coming. Waiting for us. Lined up. The best we did was bust away. Defeated. It's over. It's under. It's done."

"Does it have to be?" said Maud.

"I just told you," Oscar said, "my army lost. The rats were waiting for us," he said again. Very slowly, like he was hefting the heaviest of hurt hearts, he hoisted his eyes. "Wasn't you who told them, was it?" he asked.

"Is that what you think?"

"I don't want to."

"Why would you think I'd do that?"

"You're . . . a rat."

"You got to learn to rate your rodents right," said Maud. "It wasn't me. It so happens it was your own Uncle Wilkie."

Oscar sat up straight as an arrow heading to heaven. "Uncle Wilkie!" he cried. "How do you even know about him?"

"It's my job to know what to know when it's worth the knowing," said Maud.

Oscar shook his head. "I don't believe it."

"Ask him yourself."

Oscar sank back down. That time he stayed down and deep for a long count. "That really true about my uncle?" he muttered at last.

Maud nodded.

Oscar sighed. "It don't matter," he said. "You rats have taken over."

"Hey, just because my old man is crooked," Maud said fiercely, "don't mean I am."

That made Oscar sit up again. "Your father? Who's your father?"

"They call him Duds."

"The boss of the rats? He's *your* father?"

Maud nodded.

Acting like a yo-yo on the limp, Oscar dropped down again. "Hate to hear it," he managed to say.

"Why?"

"I had . . . hopes. . . ." He left the sentence hanging high—with no place to go.

Maud looked down at him. "I'm sorry too," she whispered. And what she did, see, was put a soft paw on his shoulder.

The power of that paw spoke a pound of passion. "You're being very kind," Oscar said.

"I want to be," Maud whispered.

"Even though I've been beaten?" asked Oscar.

"Even though."

"Forever?" he said, looking into her beautiful rat's eyes.

"Forever," she returned with a soulful squint into his soft squirrel eyes.

Which, as I heard it, was just about when Molly, who was listening all the time behind her counter, called out, "Hey, anyone want a glass of sap?"

Chapter the Thirty-fourth
THE CHALLENGE

WHILE MOLLY KEPT to herself behind the counter, Maud and Oscar just sat there, paw to paw, talking more with eyes than tongues. It was only after a while that Maud said, "Oscar, I think I know how you can still win."

Oscar shook his head. "Not possible."

"Maybe," said Maud. "But have you considered baseball?"

"What you talking about?"

"My father loves baseball."

"It hurts to hear something nice about him."

"According to your friend Sam," Maud went on, "you love the game too. And you're good."

"Maybe."

"Do you have a good team?"

"Ain't nobody better than the Central Park Green Sox."

"Well, then," said Maud. "Here's what you should do: Challenge my old man to a game."

Oscar looked at her with big eyes.

"Tell him if he wins he can have the park."

"And if we win?"

"He'll trot on back downtown."

"Think it'll work?"

"The only thing, Oscar," said Maud, "you really got to win."

Oscar thought hard. "I got everyone but my ace pitcher."

Maud nodded. "Arty Bigalow?"

Oscar shook his head. "The one and only."

"He's gone," said Maud. "Forever."

"I guess."

"Can't you win without him?"

Oscar shook his head again.

"But if you don't play," said Maud, "you'll lose the park for sure."

"I know."

Then Maud took a deep breath and said, "If I promise to get you a pitcher as big and bad as Bigalow, will you play?"

"Where you going to find one?"

"Trust me," said Maud.

And that's when Oscar said the first of his I do's.

So early next morning, Duds was strolling around the terrace by the angel fountain, near the Lake. Feeling good about his victory from the night before, the big rat was puffed up big as a baloney balloon. Pilwick was trailing after him.

"I'm telling you, Pilwick," said Duds, "beating them park saps was a snap and a song. Which is a combination I happen to like. They run off so fast they left their shadows behind. Know what I'm thinking?"

"No, Boss."

"Now that we beat them pugs, we can take over the rest of the park easy. Build a fence around it. Anyone wants in, they first hands over a cute coin."

"Take some work," said the possum.

"We got time. And talking about time, you find Maud yet?"

"Nope," said Pilwick.

"How come?"

"How come what?"

"How come a smart possum like youse can't find a dumb girl like that?"

"Maybe she ain't so dumb."

Duds popped a paw into his pocket, poking round for his pistol. He was just about to pull it when a rat ran out of his office.

"Hey, Boss," this rat said. "There's this squirrel wants to see you."

"If it's that Uncle Wilkie, tell him I don't need him anymore."

"No, Boss, it's a different one. Says he's the mayor of Central Park."

"The mayor? What's he want?"

"To talk to you."

"You know anything about this?" Duds asked Pilwick.

Pilwick turned away.

Duds stared at the possum like he was considering constructing a hole into his back. Then he turned to the rat. "Bring him in."

So the rat went off and brought back Oscar.

Oscar was dressed to the nines, you know, that light, white cotton suit, shiny shoes with spats, a loose blue bow tie, and a ripe red rose on his jacket lapel.

Duds looked him up. Looked him down. Looked him around. "You really the mayor of Central Park?"

"That's what they call me," said Oscar, trying hard not to be nervous.

"Hey, Pal, youse can call yourself a moose on the loose for all I care. You come to surrender?"

Oscar pulled himself up. "I'm here to offer you a challenge."

"A challenge!" Duds looked around like he lost something. "Youse gotta be kidding. What kind of change you got to challenge me with?"

"A baseball game."

That took Duds down a bit. I mean, it wasn't what he expected. "What you talking about?"

So Oscar said, "Central Park Green Sox against you downtown rats. We're the home team. You're the visitors."

"Yeah, but what for?"

"If we win, you dance back downtown. All of you. If you win, you can take over the park."

"And all of youse leave?" said Duds.

"If you win."

"Course we will," said Duds.

"Then that's the deal," said Oscar. "And since I'm the mayor of Central Park, what I say goes."

"How about if when we win, I get your ball team too?"

"We're going to win."

"But if you don't?"

"Okay. Sure."

So what does Duds do, he grabbed Pilwick over by his coat sleeve. "I got me a witness."

"That's fine with me," said Oscar.

Duds grinned. "I like it," he said. "I like it a lot." He held out a paw. Oscar shook it.

"Deal," said Duds.

"Deal," said Oscar.

"When's the game?"

"Saturday. Noon."

"Noon is none too soon for me, Pal," said Duds.

Oscar left.

Duds turned to Pilwick. "I guess I need to keep you around awhile," he said. "You're my chief witness."

"Whatever you say, Boss."

"I did say."

Chapter the Thirty-fifth
THE BIG GAME

THE GAME WAS set for Saturday right at noon. It was to be played at the Ball Grounds, not far from Central Park's Artisans' Gate over to Fifty-ninth Street.

Oscar, being the home-team manager as well as the mayor of Central Park, made sure the diamond was polished to perfection.

His team was mostly set. Behind the plate was Ulysses S. Crackover, better known as Reds. Cyrus X. Furdly held first base. Thaddeus (Twilly) Twilliger was at second. Canfield Roach was set for third. Oscar, of course, was short. The outfield was Parker Baladoni and Big Benny Ludwig, right along with Engelbert Maxamillion.

Archibald (Corny) Cornwallis was coaching from third base, while Sam Peekskill—shoulder set in a sling—was first-base coach.

So there it was. The only player missing was the pitcher.

Oscar was nervous. True, Maud had told Oscar not to worry. Said she had a plan about a pitcher. And though he was busting to trust her, he was tight and tense.

As for Duds, he culled his club from his gang and tagged the team the Downtown Duds. And of course, Duds was manager.

There were two umpires: one, picked by Oscar, was the screech owl. He was parked behind the plate. The other ump, a crocodile friend of Duds's, was roaming around second base, giving each and all a crowded grin.

Word had got out about the big game. So that meant there were lots of voters jostling to see the joust. In fact, along the first-base line, park voters had packed themselves in.

Along the third-base line was Duds's rat gang.

There were only three non-rats with the rats. One was Uncle Wilkie, who didn't feel too great being there.

There was also the police commissioner, Titus P. Snibly, whose tongue was still slipping in and out.

Standing around, just to keep things in order, were a few bulldog cops.

As for old possum Pilwick, he stood a little behind Duds, next to Bertha. Bertha hadn't wanted to come, because baseball bored her. But Pilwick told her she'd best be there.

Then there was the goat, Mr. Van Blunker, who had gotten into his old Downtown Dutchmen suit. Hanging over him was Evelina Telesforo, her wattles wafting with excitement. Even Oscar's ma was there, shading herself with a big black umbrella.

Molly the mole was there too, polishing baseballs.

Only one not in sight was Maud.

The tension was as high as a twenty-story tower, and it didn't get any less when the screech owl let loose with "Play ball!"

And then, who should come out from around the crowd? None other than Maud herself. But this time she was dressed in no nursing uniform. She was wearing the Green Sox suit. Only one exception: Instead of green trousers, she'd decked herself out in bulging green bloomers.

When Oscar saw her, he could hardly believe his eyes.

When Duds saw her, he could hardly believe *his* eyes.

He turned to yell at Pilwick. But Pilwick wasn't there no more. He had slipped sides and was standing next to his friend the goat. An old cap with a double *D* was on him.

And when Bertha done do the same, Duds yelled at her, but she paid him no mind.

In fact, there wasn't nothing for Duds to do but have a private fit and a half there and then. For, of course, a manager can do a whole lot of things, but pulling a pistol ain't part of the game.

And when all the rest of the teams—both sides—seen Maud, they couldn't believe their eyes neither. But the crowd from Central Park started to yowl and cheer. While over on the rat side, they started to bat around some boos.

Anyway, Maud, pert and pretty, walked herself out to the pitcher's mound. Oscar ripped over to talk to her, even as Reds trotted up from behind the plate. Then they had one of those conferences they always do in baseball—only this one was different.

"Sweetest Maud," said Oscar, "I know you are the pick of the perfect, but can you pitch?"

"I was taught by Artemus Bigalow," she said. "He might have been the worst. But some of him was best."

So Oscar said, "Give the gal the ball," and trotted back to his shortstop spot.

Next thing the screech owl yelled, "Play ball!" And Stuey the rat—remember him?—he stood up at the plate.

Maud wound up, wafted a wad of spit onto the ball, kicked, and sent a pitch popping toward the plate.

What she threw was Arty Bigalow's patented nifty knuckleball-spitball combo, which floated to the plate like a nervous butterfly with a history of hiccoughs.

Stuey, who had dug in, swung like a heavy hinge, and when he missed by a mile, the game was switched to on.

Maud was good, but she wasn't perfect. Few are. The Green Sox did their bit, and to tell the truth, so did the rats.

Which meant it all came down to a 5–5 tie in the eighth inning. And if things were tense before, they were about to get ten times worse, which was close to a hundred.

What happened next was that at the top of the ninth the rats went ahead, on a bunt, and two steals (which is something Duds liked to do). True, it included a decision at third by the crocodile, which seemed, to most who saw it, more toothful than truthful.

Try arguing with a crocodile.

Oscar could see that Maud was getting discouraged. So he trotted over to the mound. He told her that he loved her, which he hoped she knew, and love might be love but what she really needed to do was strike the next guy out.

Which she did.

Then it was the bottom of the ninth, with the Central Park Green Sox down by one.

What happened next was the mouse Engelbert

Maxamillion led off with a shot that was more than double his size—and left him sitting on second.

At which point Duds yelled to his team, "Anybody makes an error, I'll shoot him." Which of course only made them nervous as a dime standing on edge.

Sure enough, when Parker Baladoni popped a poke toward third, the rat at the hot spot bobbled the ball. So now there were park players perched on first and third.

The next up was Crackover, who worked himself a walk. So what we got were bases loaded.

And of course—this wouldn't be much of a tale if it wasn't all tied tight as a tick—that brought up Oscar himself, the mayor of Central Park.

The park fans were standing and cheering.

The rat fans were standing and booing.

And what Oscar did, he looped one as far as the Lake itself, where it plopped in the water and was forever lost.

It was a home run is what it was: So, the Green Sox won their game and with it Central Park.

Chapter the Thirty-sixth

LAST BITS AND BITES

Now, THERE AIN'T a whole lot more I can say, except I need to say it anyway. Which is good, because I always think long endings in big books are like ice-cream cones with the ice cream already licked off—and nothing left but that soggy waffle bit.

Anyway, Duds and his gang didn't just go back to downtown; they went all the way to Brooklyn, down by the Gowanus Canal.

I'd like to tell you Duds left off his life of crime, but I'm not so sure. What I do know is he made a lot of money somehow, and bought himself that National League Brooklyn baseball team. He changed their name to the Dudgers. But then some good Brooklyn folks complained, so Duds did a deal, offering to change one letter. That made them the Dodgers.

Oh, yeah. Uncle Wilkie. He had to leave Manhattan and go with Duds. Last I heard he was writing a book about the life of Duds.

As for Mr. Pilwick, he stayed in Manhattan. What's more, he's got a room in Mr. Van Blunker's Fifth Avenue house, along with Evelina Telesforo.

Artemus Bigalow did go west. Remember that horse that Duds told him to buy? Well, Arty rode to Hollywood and became a cowboy star.

Oscar's ma—Mrs. Westerwit—she got herself a new house. It's a tree on the west side of the park near Sixty-sixth Street. She serves a terrific tea on Tuesdays.

Sam Peekskill's shoulder got better, but sad to say he never was the same player he used to be.

Regarding the rest of the park voters, with Duds done, life went right back to regular doings. Except, as time went on, if you counted all the voters who had said they been at that midnight battle, it's amazing they didn't win a victory.

As for Oscar and Maud . . . sure, they married up. She became a nurse at Bellevue Hospital.

Though Oscar stayed mayor, more than anything,

he gave his game to Maud, and she gave her heart to him, and as much as I ever heard, they went into extra innings.

Fact, Oscar was the best mayor Central Park ever had. I was told they even made a statue of him. If they did, I never found it. But then, I never had time to look. New York City is a busy place.